Dedication

Because I was heartbroken when my big brother started school, my mother spent time reading to me and my love affair with books began. Books have been my haven and escape ever since. So I dedicate this book to all those whose favorite place is in the pages of a book. And to Mum and Dad for reading to me way back when.

Katie

❧ BOOK 3 ❧

Orphan Train Series

Wendy May Andrews

☙❧

Sparrow Ink
www.sparrowink.com

ISBN - 978-1-7750069-7-8

www.wendymayandrews.com

Stay in touch with Wendy May Andrews
and forthcoming publishing news.

Sign up for her biweekly newsletter

Acknowledgements

Thanks go to my beta readers: Marlene, Suzanne, Monique, and Alfred – your zeal for my stories and making them better makes my heart happy.

Thank you to my editor, Julie Sherwood, I love working with you. Any mistakes left are my fault, not hers.

Thank you too to my online communities full of wonderful readers and writers who help me with research or cheer me on.

And sincere thanks need to also go to my husband for being my everything – friend, partner, companion, web guru, formatter, idea sounding board, counterpart. You're the best, Mr. Andrews.

Chapter One

Katie walked along the dusty trail reveling in the sweet clutch of the small, warm hand holding tightly to her own, careful not to reveal how much it meant to her by holding on too tightly. One of the few little girls to have been included in the group of train orphans, little Annie still hadn't found a family to take her in. While Katie wanted her to find a good home, she was secretly glad that she could spend a little more time with her. If only she were in a position to take her herself. She swallowed the sigh that pushed to escape. She smiled instead.

"Good day, ladies," the gentleman lifted his hat slightly and bent a little, as though to bow to them.

Frowning, Katie wanted to ignore him, but Annie, usually so shy, stopped in her tracks to gaze at the man. Katie couldn't very well carry on without her.

"Hello," the little girl answered simply and continued staring at the stranger.

When he crouched down to be on her level, Katie's heart softened ever so slightly before she hardened her resolve once more. It didn't matter that he was approachable. Being handsome as the devil with his thick dark hair, clear gray eyes, and strong cheekbones and jaw line was a drawback if you asked her. Made her think he was in league with the Dark Knight to be that good looking. He probably had a black heart to go with it. She wanted to snatch Annie up into her arms and run away while babbling a mantra of "handsome men are devils you must avoid," over and over. But that would never do. She gritted her teeth and bore the silence that felt like it stretched for eons but was probably merely a couple heartbeats in length.

1

When it seemed like neither of the females were going to say anything further, the stranger broke the silence, directing his words toward Annie. "You must be new around here, young miss. I haven't yet had the pleasure of making your acquaintance."

"I just arrived," she answered, her small chest seeming to fill with importance at the adult attention. She wasn't used to men being around; it was usually only women who worked at the orphanage, except for the laborers, and they never paid her much mind anyway.

Katie swallowed the lump in her throat when she saw the depth of fascination in the little girl's gaze. Katie again suppressed the urge to snatch her away. She didn't want to develop the reputation as a madwoman in her new town. She couldn't flee from every stranger. She was new in town — everyone was a stranger.

"Welcome to Bucklin. My name is Dr. Wyatt Jeffries."

Annie's eyes grew wide at his words, and she stepped closer to Katie. "I don't like doctors," she declared firmly.

Katie pursed her lips together to prevent a grin from spreading across her face. She needn't scare the girl off about this man; he'd done it all by himself. She avoided his curious gaze as the doctor looked at her for some sort of explanation. She didn't oblige.

She realized she ought not to brush past him wordlessly. If he truly was the town doctor, she would probably have to encounter him from time to time about town. She would never seek out his services, of course, but she didn't want to appear to be a total boor.

"We really ought to be on our way, Dr. Jeffries. It was nice of you to welcome us. Good day."

With those words, she hurried away with Annie tucked firmly beside her. She ignored his words that followed her.

"But you didn't even tell me your names."

Her strides were purposeful and Annie had to almost run to keep up. Katie tried to talk herself into a state of calm once more. She needn't drag the child for the next mile while she worked off her fidgets.

"Well that was too bad, wasn't it, Sweet Pea? What are the chances of us running into a doctor here? I wasn't even sure if a town this size would have a doctor."

"He seemed nice until he told us that, didn't he?"

"It wasn't really long enough for me to decide," Katie answered carefully, not wanting to put her own issues onto the child. "But never mind about him, we're almost to the mercantile. I can't wait to see what they have."

"Do you think they might have some lemon drops?" The child's hopeful tone put a grin back onto Katie's face.

"There is a strong possibility. And an even stronger chance that I'll buy you a couple. But you mustn't spoil your appetite for dinner."

The little girl skipped along beside her, delighted at the prospect of such a treat. Katie's heart turned over. The poor child had faced so much trouble and loss in her six short years. It was a marvel that she could still delight in such simple things as the prospect of a treat. Katie resolved to do all in her power to ensure the little girl was soon settled into a happy, secure home. How she would do that was still to be determined, but she would worry about that later. Now she had the delightful prospect ahead of her of exploring the local general store. She knew it would be nothing like what they had in New York, but she was anxious to see what there was. It would help her know where to begin with this new life she had set for herself. She was determined to make it a success despite her rocky reaction to any men she encountered. With time, surely that would pass. Or she would at least be able to hide it better.

With a firm tread and her chin lifted to enforce her determination, Katie stepped briskly through the open door and felt her eyes widen as she looked around. She suppressed a giggle. It was nearly everything you could find in New York but on a much smaller scale, all packed into one open room. She could barely take it all in there was such a variety of items on display.

"Lemon drops," Annie whispered reverentially.

The little girl's tone surprised a giggle out of Katie's throat despite its tightness. She took a deep, fortifying breath. Determined to show the little girl a good time, Katie kept the smile pinned to her face, maintained her relaxed grip on the girl's hand, and began to stroll around the room.

"We'll get the candies when we're ready to go," she told the eager youngster. "We can't eat them until we've paid for them, anyway."

The store owner must have overheard because his kind smile encompassed them as he beckoned them closer. "Surely you can have one for now to tide you over," he said with a wink as he pulled one of the coveted candies out of the case and dropped it into Annie's eagerly outstretched hand.

Her eyes round as saucers, Annie looked from Katie to the kindly shopkeeper. "Thank you ever so much, mister." There was no way she was going to refuse his largesse. She popped the candy into her mouth and graced both adults with a wide grin.

"That was kind of you, thank you," Katie murmured, trying to ignore his questioning gaze, knowing he probably wanted to chat. She didn't have very much experience with towns and villages, but she had no trouble interpreting the look of curiosity painted on his face. Despite the long train ride, she still hadn't fully settled on what she would be willing to share about herself. She offered a polite smile, took Annie's hand once more, and proceeded to meander around the store.

There was an amazing array of articles. Not the variety of each type that you would find in New York, of course, but she was surprised to see that she couldn't think of anything she might want or need that wasn't present in the crowded emporium. No doubt the presence of train service made keeping the store stocked that much easier, despite how far they were from a real city. It reaffirmed for her that she had made a good decision when she thought to settle here. She felt the first hint of assurance settle into her mind, and with it, her shoulders relaxed incrementally.

Looking over the many bolts of fabric, Katie nodded to herself. She would be able to set herself up as a seamstress. Hopefully there wasn't already one in the town, or if there was, they wouldn't make too much fuss about her efforts to get some business. Surely the town was big enough that anyone who wanted to start a business could do so.

Katie glanced back at the shopkeeper. She would have to discuss with him whether or not he could offer her a discount on fabric since she would obviously be a frequent customer. Her stomach knotted itself up at the thought. Perhaps another day. It was enough that she had ventured out this far. With a sigh, she picked out the few items she absolutely required and made her way to the counter.

"And a small bag of the lemon candies, please, sir."

The shopkeeper, although seemingly pleasant, hadn't said anything as he added up her purchases. Katie appreciated that he was sufficiently perceptive to realize she didn't want to talk. *Maybe people here mind their own business,* she thought to herself with an inward smile.

"Have a good day," was all he said as the two girls left the store with a wave.

Annie cast her a sideways glance. "Did you like the store?"

"I did, did you?"

The little girl shrugged. "There were too many things for my eyes to see. I'll have to go again to decide for sure."

This prompted a chuckle from Katie. "Why is that?"

All Annie did at first was shrug again. She lapsed into silence for a moment, as though pondering the depth of the question. "I s'pose it's nice that there was so much stuff. But I think it's better if there aren't so many things. That store made me think of a New York street. All crowded and colourful. I like it better here."

"Do you really?"

The girl nodded vigorously.

"I'm so happy to hear that. I would have thought you would be a little bit homesick for the familiarity of the city."

"Everything I was used to was already gone," the girl answered, her wistful tone making Katie's heart ache.

"Of course," Katie replied and squeezed her hand. "This will soon become familiar, I hope."

The child's sunny smile appeared in response.

Katie marvelled at how resilient the child was. She had lost everything. No parents or siblings. Only strangers to care for her in the orphanage. And now a strange new place to call home. Hopefully a nice family would soon claim her as their own. The thought made Katie's heart clench once more, even though it would be the best thing for the child. Again, she wished she could claim her herself. But she shoved the useless thought away. The child needed a mother and a father. Not a broken widow like herself.

"Shall we go sit on the edge of the planks to eat our candies while we watch to see what there is to see?"

Annie's vigorous nod was accompanied by a grin.

Chapter Two

Wyatt Jeffries watched the woman and her daughter walk away. He stood stock still with his heart hammering. He ought to sit down. There was clearly something wrong with him. It didn't take his doctor's degree to know it wasn't healthy for a man's heart to hammer at such a speed.

His eyes followed the pair as they made their way into the mercantile. He ought to be continuing on his way. Mrs. Jenkins' boils wouldn't be getting better on their own. And she certainly wouldn't thank him for dawdling.

Shaking his head wouldn't rid it of the image of the lovely brunette with her crooked smile and wary eyes. The color in her cheeks had proclaimed her vigorous health despite her cold reception to his greeting. Even though she was a tiny little woman, she had seemed to be brimming with life as he watched her interacting with the child before he had interrupted them. Wyatt would guess she was in her early twenties. He wondered who her husband was.

"Surely you're committing several sins at once by thinking about how attractive another man's wife is," he muttered to himself as he set off in the direction of Mrs. Jenkins and her boils.

The afternoon pressed on as he made his rounds of the few patients he needed to visit. He tried to give his undivided attention to each person as they deserved, but he found his mind returning again and again to the mystery woman and the little girl.

"What's ailing you today?" Mr. Hunter asked, as he peered over his spectacles at the doctor, making Wyatt's face heat up.

He tried for innocence. "I am feeling perfectly fit today, thank you for asking."

Mr. Hunter chortled. "That ain't what I meant, and well you know it."

Wyatt's face felt even hotter as he tried to brazen it out. "I apologize, sir, if I have not given you sufficient focus today."

"Get on with you, boy, that ain't my concern. I jest thought you was troubling with something, and I was being neighborly. But if you don't feel like sharing, I s'pose I'll have to mind my own affairs."

Wyatt knew his face was aflame at this point and appreciated that the old codger before him didn't laugh at his expense, despite the twitch of his lips. He made an effort to apologize again, but the old man brushed it away.

"You were right, my thoughts are elsewhere today, but they seem to be muddled, and I wouldn't be able to put them into words, even if I wanted to."

The older man finally seemed satisfied with this explanation, nodding sagely. "That happens to the best of us at times, young man, you needn't be so embarrassed by it."

Wyatt flushed again, cursing his pale skin that gave away his every discomfort. But to his relief, the older man just chuckled. Closing his bag as he got to his feet and willing away his embarrassment, he cleared his throat and strived for a professional manner. "Your wound is healing nicely, Mr. Hunter. I should be able to remove the stitches the next time I stop in to see you."

This reminded the old man of his initial complaint. "I don't see why you can't do it now. Cursed stitches. I can't do nothing with them in there."

"Well, it would be best if you don't do much for at least a week or two even after their out, so with an attitude like you've got, I might have to leave them in a little longer than planned if you don't plan to behave."

The disbelieving look on the oldster's face forced a chuckle out of Wyatt.

"You wouldn't be so mean spirited, would you, Doc?"

"See that you behave for the next couple of days, and we'll discuss it when I see you again."

"Maybe I'll hide the next time you call round," Mr. Hunter muttered, forcing another chuckle from the doctor.

"You could do that, but then what would happen with your stitches? And what if you were to develop an infection?"

The older man paled at his words, making Wyatt regret them. "Never mind, Mr. Hunter. I will be back in a few days. You will be perfectly fine in the meantime. Just try to keep the bandage clean and dry, and everything will be fine, have no fear."

Wyatt tied his bag onto the back of his saddle and swung his leg over his sturdy horse, grateful for the animal's steady personality. With how distracted he had been that day, he was lucky the horse hadn't wandered away and gotten him lost. Thinking about his distraction led his thoughts back to the source of that distraction.

The small child had seemed to be the picture of health. And her mother as well. The lovely color on her cheekbones proclaimed how well her blood was circulating from the rigors of their walk through town. The mother had been a little on the thin side, he mused, but the child had been exactly the right size for what appeared to be a five-year-old girl. He frowned as he thought a little more about the two strangers, wondering who they belonged to. He thought he knew everyone in the small town. Of course, the little girl had said they were new to town, but he wondered briefly which of the men they belonged to.

The mother's reception had certainly contrasted with the child's until the girl realized he was a doctor. He wondered if he had guessed accurately about her age. Her face didn't have a single wrinkle or line to mar its perfection, although her eyes had seemed shadowed, as though she had seen too much in her short years. Wyatt sighed. He could relate too well to that.

Giving his head a shake, he tried to pull his thoughts away from woman and child. It wasn't seemly to be thinking so much about some other man's family. In his years as a doctor, it had never happened to him before, and he wouldn't allow it to last for long. He urged his horse into a gallop, hoping the wind rushing by his ears would whisk away his troubled thoughts.

He forced himself to consider the patients he had seen that day. He had made brief notes after each visit, but he really ought to write more details and plan what to do for each of them in the future. He was particularly concerned about Mrs. Jenkins' boils. If she didn't do a better job of keeping them clean, she was sure to get a terrible infection. He didn't feel equipped to look after her properly in her home if that was to happen, but she had already been adamant about not wanting to visit him in his office. The poor old woman barely ever left her home. He would have to prevail upon her family members to help her out a bit more. That probably wouldn't go over very well with Mrs. Jenkins, but it was entirely possible that her life was at stake, so there weren't many options. He would rather suffer her anger than have her death on his conscience. But these thoughts brought him back to Mr. Hunter and his teasing when Wyatt's mind had been occupied with the pretty young mother rather than where it ought to have been, with his patient.

Wyatt was relieved when his house came into view. His chest swelled with pride whenever he looked at it. It was everything he had ever wanted in a house. Now all he needed to do was fill it with a loving wife and a few children, and his life would be complete. A vibrant, healthy wife, he reminded himself. One that would be able and happy to bear and raise his children. He shook the thoughts from his mind once more as he reached his small stable.

After doing the necessary ministrations for his horse, he grabbed his bag and headed to the house. As he stepped into the front entrance, he paused when his eyes snagged on the small portrait of Patricia. His heart clenched at the familiar sight. He really shouldn't have put it there. He should have left it in Boston with the rest of her things. But somehow that felt cold and heartless. One more thing to push to the back of his mind. He continued to the kitchen, dropping his bag by the table before going to the stove to boil some water. A good cup of coffee would fortify him to get through the rest of his paperwork for the day.

ℰℭ

"That sigh sure sounded heartfelt."

Katie smiled at her friend's words. "Sorry, Mel. I'm feeling a little melancholy this evening."

"That's nothing to be sorry for," Mel replied. "Would you care to discuss it?"

"There isn't really much to discuss," Katie began. "I spent the day with Annie today."

Mel's steady, understanding gaze made Katie falter in her speech. Her throat clogged with the threat of tears, much to her disgust. She had given up on tears long ago. Katie swallowed hard to rid herself of the unwelcome sensation. Melanie hadn't stopped watching her, so Katie felt obliged to continue.

"Do you think they would let me keep her?"

Melanie's gaze didn't falter even though her kind smile dimmed slightly. "They might, if the poor dear doesn't get spoken for soon. But do you really feel that you're in a position to care for her?"

Katie looked around their small home. "Would you be willing to have her here? I know that would probably be asking too much of you. We're a little cramped with Cassie here, too."

"I doubt Cass will be with us for too much longer," Mel began, "but space isn't really what I was concerned about. If it came to space, you could share your room with Annie, I would imagine. And she's a sweet child. She wouldn't be too much trouble, I'm sure. But you would have to be responsible for her expenses. I don't know if either of us is fully prepared to provide for ourselves, let alone taking on responsibility for another. I'm sorry to be cold about it, but I'm not prepared to take it on right now. I need to make sure I feel secure for myself first."

"No, no, Mel, I swear to you, I'm not asking for you to take on any responsibility, just as long as you would be willing to let me have her here. That, in itself, would be a big help." She paused in thought for a moment before continuing. "It's probably a foolish thought, but I just want it so much. I hope that isn't selfish of me. I cannot say for sure if it is in her best interests for me to take her on. A child really ought to have a mother and a father. But surely I would be better than letting her languish in the hands of a custodian that I cannot say I am fully convinced even cares about the wellbeing of the children." When it looked as though Mel was going to object, Katie hurried to continue. "Even Cassandra is concerned about the children."

Mel grinned. "Cass is a special case who has never witnessed the realities of life before, so she isn't the most reliable of supports for your argument. But I don't completely disagree with you. And I think Annie would be lucky to have someone as caring as you look after her.

My only concern is that you haven't yet established yourself here. I don't think you could live with yourself if you took her on and then couldn't provide for her."

Melanie's kind tone threatened her emotional control again, and Katie frowned to push the feelings away. Perhaps she was foolish to even consider it. Mel's concerns were valid. But the remembered feeling of holding the little girl's hand and listening to her chatter made Katie feel distinctly that she needed to at least try.

"I will see about putting up some sort of advertisements around town for our sewing and alterations. I haven't seen too very many women around, but surely there must be a need for seamstresses in a town of this size."

"I actually have already found us one customer. I almost forgot to tell you. Mrs. Spencer. She helps her husband run the mercantile."

"Oh, I was in the mercantile this afternoon with Annie."

"Did you meet Mrs. Spencer?"

"No, but her husband seemed like a nice enough man."

Mel grinned over Katie's grudging tone, but chose not to comment. "Perhaps you were there at the exact time I was speaking to her," she surmised. "She's a lovely woman with the biggest, blonde, curly hair I have ever seen. She was telling me that with the growth of their business, she hasn't the time to even think about doing any sewing herself but that she is in desperate need of several new articles. So we should get a fair bit of business from her. And she could end up being walking advertisement for us, seeing how visible she would be at the store."

Katie offered her friend a shrewd glance. "So you offered her a significant discount, didn't you?"

"Well, under the circumstances, it seemed wise. I would think we'll be able to negotiate an arrangement with them for getting our supplies. And if she is happy with us, she will be eager to recommend us to her own patrons."

"You don't need to convince me, Mel, I can see the wisdom in it. I just hope lots of business rolls in quickly so that I can speak with Mrs. Parker about Annie."

Mel's smile returned to the understanding state that was grating on Katie's nerves. "It's a rather circular process, isn't it?"

Katie's smile was rueful. "It would seem so." She lapsed into silence for a moment before sighing again. "Well, we should have an idea soon how much business we are likely to get. I will have a word with Mrs. Parker tomorrow about whether or not they would even consider me. It would be better to know right off if it's not even possible before I get my heart completely set on it, anyway."

"That sounds like the course of wisdom."

Mel's sage tone brought a chuckle out of Katie.

Katie got lost in thought for a moment as she reminisced about how far they'd come. It seemed like only yesterday they had met while volunteering at the Foundling Hospital in New York City. It was hard to believe it had been two years already. In some ways, it felt like only days had passed. In other ways, it was a different lifetime. Their volunteer work with the orphans had seen them escorting groups on the train out to farm towns to be adopted. Mrs. Parker, the director of the orphanage, was a wonderful older woman, who seemed impervious to the emotional toll it was taking on some of the younger women. Katie and Melanie hadn't been able to do it any longer and had decided to stay in the town when they brought this latest batch of orphans to their new lives. It had been the best decision either of them had ever made.

Chapter Three

While Katie hadn't originally planned on joining Melanie in the sewing business, they had quickly decided it would be for the best when things had settled down soon after they had arrived in Bucklin. Katie had thought she was going to be the town's new teacher, but when that opportunity disappeared, Mel had offered a partnership. It was turning out to be for the best. Melanie did not enjoy dealing with the clients, and Katie found that she really enjoyed it. And they both enjoyed the work. Doing it together was just that much more fun.

Mrs. Spencer was a dream client. Not overly demanding but knew exactly what she wanted, generous in her praise, and generous in her placement of orders as well. They were kept busy with all the items she was requesting. At first, Katie wasn't happy about the discount they had offered her, but Mr. Spencer had been generous in the discount he offered them on their materials, so it was all working out well. Mrs. Spencer was so pleased with her new clothes that she took to wearing them immediately and was quick to tell everyone where they had come from. Before they knew it, the two women were almost overwhelmed with business. Katie had to work to keep the grin on her face within bounds as she set out to visit another potential client to discuss what she was looking for and to see if they could agree on service.

Katie visited with Annie regularly. She was torn between considering it a risk for the child to become attached to her rather than her potential future parents and the sadness of leaving the poor child to languish on her own without any special adult attention. Mrs. Parker hadn't expected it take so long to find someone to take the youngster, and was itching to return to New York.

"You can be sure I'll not encourage Mr. Brace to be sending girls out here in the future. She is a dear, but if she cannot be placed, there's no sense in sending any more out this way. We've never had this kind of trouble in other towns or cities before," Mrs. Parker had mused. "I wonder if it's just a strange coincidence or if it's how far west we are. Being a bit more primitive, maybe they just don't see how much of an asset a daughter can be."

"And the town will eventually need women for all the men these boys are going to grow up to be," Katie added with a smile as she watched Annie playing. They were keeping their voices low, not wanting the little girl to overhear their discussion. "I do hope you can find a nice family for her soon."

"Me, too," Mrs. Parker's agreement was heartfelt. "If she were a boy, I'd leave her for Mr. McDonald to care for and be on the next eastbound train, but I just cannot leave her with him on her own. I'm not even comfortable with the man, let alone leaving a little girl in his care."

Katie chewed her lip as she thought of the burly placement manager and how unsuitable it would be to leave the little girl with him. "You could always let me adopt her." It wasn't the first time she had brought this up.

She hated the pitying look Mrs. Parker cast her way. "You know Mr. Brace is particular about the children going to families, Katie. You're a dear for caring about her, but you must see that it would be better for her to join a family."

"I do see that, but if there isn't a family for her, I'm better than letting her languish alone or taking her back to the orphanage, aren't I?"

Mrs. Parker patted her hand. "Katie, dear, you are lovely, and it is certainly not anything personal. I would give her to you in a heartbeat if you had a husband."

Katie grimaced at the words, making Mrs. Parker smile in response. "I'll tell you what. I'll telegraph Mr. Brace and ask him for a decision. If we don't have a family for little Annie soon, I think you're right. It would be much better for her to be with you than for her not to have anyone."

Admonishing herself not to get her hopes up, Katie nodded and thanked the woman. "I'll be around again tomorrow, but I ought to get on with my appointments. Thank you for your diligence on behalf of the children, Mrs. Parker."

"Well, how sweet of you to say that, Katie. And thank you for your constant care of the little ones. Good day, Mrs. Carter."

Katie was surprised that the older woman had resorted to formalities but then realized that the manager, Mr. MacDonald, had entered the room. She couldn't grow comfortable with the man.

"Mr. MacDonald, good day," Katie acknowledged, as she left the room with a small nod. Brief but polite. Since she was trying to gain custody of the little girl, it wouldn't do to offend the placement manager, no matter how incompetent he seemed to be.

She wondered briefly if she should write to Mr. Brace herself. She didn't want to speak ill of the placement manager, but she wondered how hard Mr. MacDonald really was working to find homes for the orphans Mr. Brace's Children's Society was sending out west. Katie knew the warm-hearted philanthropist would be incensed to learn someone he trusted was failing in his duties to the children. But on the other hand, she wanted Annie for herself, and if Mr. MacDonald's incompetence made that possible, she wasn't about to complain.

Katie made her way through her day's activities in a bit of a daze. She was making every effort not to get her hopes too high that she would be allowed to keep Annie, but she couldn't seem to stop herself. She tried not to betray her rising excitement as she visited a potential client. It took effort to focus her attention on the matter at hand. She wasn't experienced enough as a seamstress not to have her mind on the subject and needed to concentrate to make sure she fully understood what the woman was looking for. Thankfully, the potential client was a kind, middle-aged woman who hadn't had a new frock in a few years and was delighted with whatever Katie had to suggest. And she had seen Mrs. Spencer's new clothes and wanted some for herself, so she was already prepared to pay whatever price Katie and Melanie named. They didn't want to take advantage of their new neighbors' desperation but they had agreed to reasonable prices that would support them comfortably without having to work all hours of every day.

There was an even bigger skip to her step as Katie walked away from the house. The woman had given her a deposit on two new frocks and a gown. Katie wasn't sure what use the woman had for it, but if she wanted a fancy gown, they would make it for her. It would actually be a pleasure to make it with Melanie.

The increase in their income made her feel that much more secure in her desire to take custody of Annie. *If Mr. Brace and Mrs. Parker allow it,* she reminded herself for maybe the twentieth time that day. It was so hard to restrain her excitement. But so little had gone her way in her adult life, she really ought to keep a firm grip on reality. It wouldn't do to hope too much or she would slip into a decline when they finally told her no.

Katie burst through her front door. "Mrs. Smith placed a larger order than I expected, and the mercantile is getting us a larger variety of fabrics so we don't have to worry about our clients running around town in identical clothing," she called out to Melanie as she shut the door.

"That's wonderful, Katie. Thank you for looking after both of those things. Are you very sure you don't mind being the one who always deals with the clients?" Melanie's tone revealed her anxieties, despite her effort to repress them.

"I'm more than certain. Your stitches are finer than mine. We're both playing to our strengths." She breezed through the small room, opening the window above the sink to allow more of the spring air into their tidy home. "Have you been outside yet? It's a gorgeous day."

Melanie admitted that she had not but then she chuckled. "You sure seem to be in a fine frame of mind. Whatever has happened to you?"

Katie grinned. "Mrs. Parker is going to ask Mr. Brace if I can adopt Annie."

Melanie's eyebrows rose, but so did the corners of her mouth. "And so you are thrilled," she stated with a laugh before sobering. "But how likely is he to say yes, do you suppose?"

Katie shrugged in an effort to demonstrate a lack of concern but couldn't help feeling uncertain and chewing her lip. "Even a widow is better than no one," she explained. "They wouldn't want to take her back to New York after dragging her out here, so Mrs. Parker said if they do not find a family for her soon, there is a good chance he will approve it. It helps that he knows me, of course." She paused, looking out the window for a moment, trying to regain control over her hopes, but then she whirled toward Melanie and exclaimed, "Oh, Mel, I know I oughtn't to hope too strongly, but I just want it to be true. I want to be a mother again. Surely they must say yes."

Melanie made a tsking sound and pulled Katie in for a quick hug. "Let us try to keep you too preoccupied to dwell on it until you can know for sure. I know you want the best for Annie, and I trust that Mrs. Parker does as well. If they can find a family to take her in, then that might be for the best, but if not, I know you will be a wonderful mother." She then briskly strode across the room. "Now let us get to work on Mrs. Smith's order. It will help you keep your mind away from your wishes and dreams."

Katie laughed. "I hope you're right, but sometimes sewing leaves little for the mind to do other than think."

Melanie grinned. "True, but not this time. You will be the one to figure out the pattern. That should keep your mind fully occupied."

Katie pulled a face but gamely set to work.

Several days passed with Katie nearly wearing herself to the bone trying hard not to dwell too much on the possibilities. They finished Mrs. Smith's order and she delivered it. "That was much quicker than I expected," the delighted client exclaimed. Katie had had to smother her smile over that. It probably wouldn't happen again.

She visited with Annie every other day. She didn't want the child to grow unreasonably attached to her if she was going to be living with a new family, but Katie couldn't bear to leave the poor child completely. It had to be difficult for the little girl, being the last one without a new family.

Finally, on Friday, when Katie arrived to see Annie, Mrs. Parker called her aside while the child was absorbed in a book Katie had brought for her.

In a low voice, the older woman asked, "Were you completely serious when you expressed an interest in adopting Annie?"

Katie had to fight not to yell. "Of course," she exclaimed in a loud whisper.

"Very well, then. Mr. Brace has agreed to allow it."

Tears welled in Katie's eyes. Mrs. Parker must have mistaken the cause. "Katie, dear, you know our hesitation was not any personal judgement against you, don't you?"

"Of course, I completely understood. I am just so thrilled that I am going to have her as my daughter. I have been trying not to hope too strongly, but it has been a challenge. Are you completely sure that I can have her?" she couldn't help but ask.

Mrs. Parker smiled at her, warm understanding spreading across her face. "I am certain. If you'd like, you can tell her the good news now."

Chapter Four

Katie made every effort not to skip as she walked beside Annie, leading her back to the little house she was sharing with Mel. She was a mom, she reminded herself. She needed to be responsible. But oh how she wanted to twirl in circles and jump for joy!

Thankfully, Cassie had already moved out, so space wouldn't be such an issue. And the little girl had only the one bag of belongings, so she wouldn't be cluttering up the place either. Katie glanced down and intercepted the apprehensive glance of the small girl.

"Are you nervous, Annie?" Katie was surprised at the possibility.

She got a slight nod in answer causing Katie to stop in her tracks and crouch down in front of her.

"Why are you nervous? We know each other quite well. Do you not want to come and live with me?" Katie hoped her disappointment didn't come through in her voice. She wanted the child to know she had a say in her future. "Would you rather stay with Mrs. Parker and keep waiting for someone else?"

Tears welled up in Annie's eyes, which made a lump form in Katie's, and she had to blink several times to keep the tears out of her own vision.

"What is it, honey? You can tell me. I promise not to get upset with whatever you have to say."

"I don't want anything bad to happen to you," Annie whispered.

Katie was shocked into silence by the little girl's concerns. "Oh, Annie, my dear, I promise you, I am in perfect health. Nothing is going to happen to me. Certainly not as a result of you coming to live with me."

Standing up, but keeping Annie's hand firmly in her grasp, Katie continued. "I had been thinking that I need to be dignified about this, but I realize now that I was mistaken. Today is a day we should be celebrating. We each have family now. We have each other. And that is something to rejoice about, don't you think?"

Annie just looked at her with wide, serious eyes. Katie felt her stomach drop with disappointment once more, but she didn't allow that to stop her. She put Annie's small bag of possessions carefully down on the ground and grabbed Annie's free hand with her own. Keeping her gaze focused on Annie's face, Katie forced herself to grin at the child, despite her insecure wish to curl up and cry. She was the adult here and she had to act like it.

"This is going to be just great, and I am so happy that we are going to stay together. Don't you think it's great?" Her gaiety, however forced, was beginning to get through to the youngster and the corners of her mouth were starting to lift. After another searching glance, the little girl finally nodded.

Katie wrinkled her nose at her and then grinned. "That wasn't very convincing."

Finally, Annie couldn't help it, a giggle escaped.

"There it is!" Katie declared, joy filling her heart. "I knew you would see reason. We are going to be the happiest pair in this town, just you wait and see." She eyed the girl with mock seriousness. "It is both our responsibility to make sure we are happy, wouldn't you agree?"

Annie again looked uncertain for a moment, and Katie regretted her words, but then the little girl giggled again and nodded. "I will do my very best, Mrs. Katie, I promise."

"As will I," Katie vowed in return. "Now, I do believe we ought to celebrate this pact by skipping all the way home."

Finally, Katie's heart nearly overflowed as full-throated laughter erupted from the youngster and she almost fell over with how vigorous her nodding was. Katie's laughter, while not quite as carefree, swelled forth to join Annie's. Tightening her grasp on one small hand, Katie picked up Annie's small bundle of possessions, and the two skipped along the road, their differing strides giving them more reason to laugh.

They were lost in their own enjoyment of the moment and didn't notice the horse and rider coming up behind them. They both jumped and spun around when the man spoke to them. Annie didn't even try to suppress her shriek, which caused the large horse to shy away. The rider quickly gained control of the animal then slid off his back.

Lifting his hat, he bowed politely. "I apologize for startling you. I should have realized the soft ground was muffling my steed's hoof beats when I saw how oblivious you seemed to my approach. I do hope you will forgive the intrusion."

Katie wanted to sweep by him and ignore him like she had the first time she and Annie had encountered the doctor, but she knew she ought not inflict her own issues upon her new charge. Annie had enough of her own emotional baggage toward doctors; Katie didn't want her distrust of men to rub off on the child. She forced a polite smile to her lips.

"We were having too much fun to pay attention to what was going on around us, sir, which wasn't all that wise, considering we are on a well-traveled road. It is surely not your fault that our inattention lead to our discomfort." She paused, seeing that he seemed to expect something more from her. "But thank you for so graciously offering an apology." She cringed when she heard the questioning tone at the end of her own sentence. Katie offered another smile in an effort to cover up her discomfort.

He lifted his hat and made another little bow while a deep chuckle came out of him and seemed to curl around Katie's stomach. "It does the heart good to see two such lovely ladies having a good time. No harm was done. But do try to be more careful in the future. I would hate for either of you to need my services."

Katie felt a momentary urge to relax and spend more time with the man. The thought made her stiffen and withdraw mentally. That would never do. She needed to end this meeting.

"Well, sir, thank you again for stopping and being so gracious about our occupation of the road. We ought to let you get on with your important work. We wouldn't want to prevent you from seeing to your patients." She congratulated herself on her handling of their exit. She hadn't even had to lie. No doubt, being the only doctor in town, he was a busy man. And it was true that she wouldn't want to keep him from visiting the sick.

The doctor looked reluctant but nodded his head before gathering up his reins and regaining his seat on the large horse. He tipped his hat to them once more. "Until we meet again," he said before riding away without another glance.

Katie felt a tremble down her spine. His words struck her as ominous. She didn't want to see the doctor ever again. Any doctor, really, but especially not a young, handsome one. Handsome men were trouble she had no interest in.

She forced aside her feelings and turned to Annie, whose large eyes were widened towards her with worry dulling their shine. Katie pinned a smile to her face.

"Wasn't that something? We were having so much fun we didn't even hear a horse coming. I suppose we ought to be a little more careful. Why don't we skip along through the grass here on the side?"

"Won't that be harder?"

Katie shrugged. "I think it will just make it more interesting. Come along now. We need to be getting home and making some dinner for ourselves. I don't know about you, but I think my tummy is going to be grumbling quite soon."

This finally brought the smile back to Annie's face, and the two hurried to Katie's house, returning to skipping as they had before. Katie's laughter was a little forced, but she was glad the child didn't appear to notice the difference.

Chapter Five

Wyatt rode away from the two females, castigating himself for once again not getting the woman's name. Which was beyond foolish since she was no doubt married, so her name was of little consequence. Except for it being neighborly, of course. He ought to know the names of everyone in the vicinity, since they could, at some point, be patients. His lips twisted with the irony. He truly hoped she would never be his patient. He doubted he would have the clinical detachment needed. And he fervently hoped she was never in a position to need a doctor anyway.

But she really was the loveliest woman he had ever seen. Oh, he'd seen more beautiful women, in cities, or when he was away for school. Women who were beautiful on the surface with fashionable clothes and their hair styled precisely. But those women rarely had anything going on behind their eyes. Their beauty was only surface deep. Whereas the woman, he still didn't even know her name, was very pretty on the surface, but also seemed to be thriving with life underneath. The rose color of her cheeks spoke of a rich vitality. He thought of Patricia, and the corners of his mouth turned down. She certainly hadn't been full of vitality. He quickly shoved the thought away.

And the little child, he thought again, changing the subject in his mind slightly. Annie. What a darling, timid, little thing she was. He wanted to scoop her up and hold her tight and reassure her that her future was sure to be bright. But she wasn't his to concern himself with.

Perhaps he could approach that fellow, Mr. MacDonald, who was arranging homes for the orphans who had arrived on the train. It would be wonderful to have a child in his life. Not that they would entrust a young, single man with a child, he surmised, even if he was the town's doctor. He really ought to look around the town and find himself a wife. He realized he didn't know of any available single women in the town, but surely some of the town folk must have sisters or cousins that could come and visit and give him the opportunity to meet a possible wife. Wyatt made a mental note to pay more attention when any patients spoke of their family. Surely they would be willing to set him up if he asked.

Making his way home, Wyatt tried not to feel lonely as he rode up the path. Perhaps he should get a pet. A dog or a cat might be nice. Surely a pet would be happy to see him when he returned. Of course, being called out at all hours of the day or night might make him a little less welcomed by a pet. *But dogs don't hold grudges,* he thought wistfully. *Cats might, though,* he reminded himself with a grin while wondering if his solitude was making him lose his mind.

At least he didn't have to worry that a pet was going hungry while he was gone for the day. His faithful horse had grazed throughout the day whenever he stopped to visit his patients. The horse had earned his hay and oats tonight, for all the work he had put in throughout the day.

Wyatt swung his leg over and climbed down. Fatigue seeped from his pores. He wondered what he could quickly cook up to eat before he climbed into bed. It would have to be another night of fried eggs on bread. Thank heaven for the chickens!

"You did a good job today, Boss." Despite his fatigue, Wyatt grinned when the large horse's ears swivelled, as though he were listening. He had to chuckle when the horse huffed and nodded his head, as though in agreement.

"Is it a tough job carrying me around all day?" When the horse shoved his head into Wyatt's chest, his laughter grew. "Seems to me that you're looking for a reward." He pushed the large head away but pulled a sweet lump out of his pocket. "It *is* your job to carry me around, but you probably deserve a treat anyway."

Wyatt pulled the saddle off and tried not to dump it with a thump. He was more tired than he ought to be, and he didn't have the usual strength in his arms. Despite his weariness, he needed to look after his horse. Picking up the brush, he set to work on the smooth coat, smiling as the horse twitched and stamped, demonstrating his enjoyment.

"Yeah, it's probably quite a relief to be done for the day, isn't it, big guy?" When the horse whickered, Wyatt shook his head. "Maybe I'm losing my mind if I'm starting to think that the best conversation I've had all day is this one."

The horse seemed to be lulled nearly to sleep by Wyatt's rhythmic strokes and he allowed his mind to drift back over the day. His thought jumped from the day to the past, never a good thing for his state of mind.

"Patricia would have loved to see how big you've gotten," he commented to the large horse. "She was determined that we ought to keep you instead of selling you when your mama surprised us by being pregnant. What did I know about training horses? I tried to reason with her. I'm a doctor, not a cowboy, I told her. But she wouldn't take no for an answer. She could be like that sometimes. You probably would have liked her. And it turns out, she wasn't completely wrong. Not that I think I had much to do with it. I think your mama must have taught you right because you turned out fairly well, and I certainly didn't know what I was doing."

The only reaction Boss had to offer to indicate he was still listening was the periodic shifting of his ears. Wyatt grinned again. "Yeah, I should probably get a dog. Then I wouldn't have to bore you with all this talk."

After one last stroke of the brush, Wyatt patted the horse's rump as he tossed the brush onto its shelf. He tossed an armload of hay in front of Boss and then put a scoop of feed in his trough after checking that there was enough water available to the horse.

It hadn't taken very long to care for the animal, but the brief interlude had been surprisingly restful. There was something so calming about animals, Wyatt mused. Much more so than people, he thought before reminding himself that he would still like to have an actual person around. Family, while quite able to make you a little crazy at times, was really at the heart of all that is good in life. And he didn't have any. You could hardly count third cousins out East. Although, he would take even them at this point, since he was beginning to annoy himself with his lonely whining. Hopefully a good night's sleep would put an end to his whiney ramblings.

He finally made his way into the house, taking his boots off at the door, as though he could still hear Patricia's command to do so.

What was it about today that made her so tenaciously stuck in his thoughts? He passed her favorite watercolor on the way to the kitchen. Is it any wonder, since her marks were still everywhere in his life? The painting of the small child reminded him of the little girl he had seen that day. Patricia would have loved her. If only he had been able to convince her to adopt.

With a sigh, Wyatt pushed away thoughts of his wife and proceeded to conclude his long day with an egg sandwich then climbed into bed. Morning was sure to come quickly with another long day to follow.

ℰᏻᏼ

The following afternoon, Wyatt was surprised to run into his mystery woman when he stopped in to check on old Mrs. Jenkins.

"I'm sorry if I've arrived at an inconvenient time, Mrs. Jenkins. I'm happy, though, to see that you have a visitor."

"Isn't it something, Dr. Jeffries? My daughter-in-law has hired this lovely young lady to make me a new dress. Sue thinks it will make me feel better. I don't know what goes through that woman's head sometimes," the cranky old lady chuckled. "As if new clothes can make me forget about these terrible sores. But having Katie here visiting me sure isn't a hardship."

Wyatt couldn't do anything but grin, which brought a wicked twinkle into the old woman's eyes. "Have you had the pleasure of meeting the town's new seamstress, doctor?"

"No, ma'am, I have not," he replied, taking the opportunity to shake the pretty brunette's hand. "Doctor Jeffries, at your service, ma'am."

He almost laughed over the comical look on the young woman's face. She had avoided introducing herself when they had first encountered one another. He wondered how she would handle Mrs. Jenkins' introduction. He wasn't left in suspense.

While offering him the briefest smile, she actually dipped into a slight curtsy, much to his surprise. "How do you do, doctor?"

Mrs. Jenkins took exception to her lack of elaboration. "Tell the man your name, girl. You couldn't do any better than snapping up the handsome single doctor." She cackled while the seamstress' face flamed.

"My name is Mrs. Kate Carter."

"Never mind with the Mrs., Kate, you know you're a widow. What you need is a fine, young husband to look after you," the older woman declared. "None better than our handsome doctor."

Wyatt wasn't sure how to put the poor woman at ease. Her face was so red, he worried for her health. But he knew from experience there was little one could do to stop Mrs. Jenkins when she was on a roll. He had thought Mrs. Carter timid, so he was surprised when she spoke up.

"Actually, Mrs. Jenkins, I do *not* need a husband to look after me. I am quite capable of taking care of myself and my new daughter on my own. I have had the experience of being married. I can assure you that I do not care to repeat it." Wyatt was affronted by her vehemence but had to smile when he observed her struggle to control the strength of her reaction. She must have realized it would not do to offend her client. She offered the old woman a sweet smile while she laid her hand gently on her arm. Wyatt wished he could feel that pleasant pressure himself, despite her declaration of having no wish to remarry.

"It is kind of you to be concerned about me and Annie, though, Mrs. Jenkins. Thank you for that." She cast a quick glance in Wyatt's direction. He would have never noticed if he hadn't been watching her so closely. He wished fervently that he didn't find her quite so charming. The lady continued talking.

"Now Mrs. Jenkins, since the doctor is here, would you prefer I come back some other time? I have no wish to invade your privacy."

"Never mind about my privacy. If you're going to be taking my measurements, you'll be seeing everything the doctor needs to look at anyway. We can kill two birds with one stone. Works out pretty convenient for me, I'd say."

Wyatt suppressed his grin at Mrs. Carter's obvious discomfort. She tried to hide it with brisk speech while she stood.

"Very well, Mrs. Jenkins. Since we no doubt do not wish to preoccupy the busy doctor, shall I help you undress?"

"You're a good girl, aren't you, Kate? Even if you have strange notions." The old woman cackled again as the color rose in the seamstress' cheeks anew. "Pull me to my feet, and we'll get this over with."

Mrs. Carter made short work of getting Mrs. Jenkins on her feet and her dress removed, leaving the older woman in a loose shift. The younger woman then looked quite uncomfortable as to what to do with herself. Mrs. Jenkins solved that.

"Make yourself useful, girl, and put the kettle on to boil. We can offer the doctor a cup of tea before he leaves."

Wyatt was torn between his desire to spend more time with the woman and wanting to put her at ease from her obvious reluctance to spend time with him. He stifled his grin and waited to see what she would do.

Her color remained high, but she did nothing besides offering the old woman a brief nod and hurrying to the stove. It was obvious she was relieved to be away from the doctor's examination. Wyatt wondered if she had an equal distaste for doctors as her daughter expressed. Or if it was just one particular doctor who made her uncomfortable.

He grinned when his eyes encountered Mrs. Jenkins' shrewd gaze. She surprised him by not saying anything, containing herself to a suggestive wiggle of her eyebrows. Wyatt winked at her but merely murmured his instructions regarding his examination. He was relieved to see that the salve he had left for her was obviously having an effect, since he was only able to apply, at best, half his attention to the matter at hand. The rest of his attention was listening for Mrs. Carter's activities in the kitchen area.

The doctor heartily wished he could watch the young woman. There was nothing more beautiful, in his opinion, than a woman bustling about the kitchen. That is where he longed for a woman of his own, in his lonely home, keeping his kitchen smelling delicious. Obviously the widowed seamstress would disagree with his viewpoint.

Wyatt finished his examination of Mrs. Jenkins just as the kettle whistled. He was surprised to see that the seamstress had placed some cookies on a plate and arranged all the fixings for tea on a tray, even though it had been obvious she didn't want to prolong her time with him. He admired her gumption, even though he disagreed with her philosophy.

ഇ൙ഇ

Katie wholeheartedly wished the doctor had timed his visit differently. If only he were old. Or ugly. Or married. Or any number of things, really. It was strange that she had encountered him, already, a number of times. There were many townspeople she had yet to meet. Ones who could be potential clients. Not handsome, single doctors who were of no use to her. She had absolutely no interest in feeling any sort of attraction to the man.

She had learned early in life that wishing things certainly did not make them happen, so she had taken a deep breath and set to the task Mrs. Jenkins had assigned her. If she made quick work of it, hopefully the doctor would move along to his next patient and she could get her client sorted in time to collect Annie from school. The poor dear had been so apprehensive about her first day, Katie certainly didn't want to be late.

"Thank you, dear," Mrs. Jenkins smiled at her as she poured her a cup of tea. "You did a good job in my kitchen, despite your independent ideas of having a career."

Katie laughed. She wasn't offended by the old woman's words. She knew her refusal to remarry was a little unusual, but this was 1854 for heaven's sake. It was perfectly acceptable for a woman to be independent and rely on herself rather than a husband.

"I consider that high praise coming from you, Mrs. Jenkins, thank you." With no desire to talk about herself and even less to show any interest in the doctor, Katie turned the subject. "Have you always lived her in Bucklin?"

"No. My dearly departed Mr. Jenkins brought me out here from the East when we married."

"Was it a big adjustment for you?"

"Probably not as much as an adjustment as you'll be going through being from the big city. I grew up on a farm, so it wasn't so different. But of course, Bucklin barely existed when I arrived, so we had to make do with no stores and no train. I came by stagecoach. It took days on end. Not like it is with the train now. We've become so modern."

Katie had to laugh again. Mrs. Jenkins was quite right. Bucklin, Missouri was nothing like New York City. If she thought this was modern, Katie shuddered to think what it was like when Mrs. Jenkins first arrived. But she couldn't say that.

"It must have been so exciting to see the changes."

"I don't know about exciting, but I guess it's been interesting," was all the cranky woman would allow.

Finally, politeness would not allow Katie to ignore the doctor any longer. She would have to talk to him.

"Have you always lived in Bucklin, Doctor Jenkins?"

"No, ma'am. I grew up not far from where Mrs. Jenkins is from, in fact. Pittsburgh, Pennsylvania. Have you ever been there?"

Katie just shook her head. "I've never been anywhere but New York until coming here."

"This is quite a change for you, then, isn't it?"

She couldn't tell if it was censure or admiration in his voice. She felt her chin rising.

"I am quite convinced that experiencing new things causes character growth." Katie didn't want to feel charmed when he grinned at her and nodded his agreement. She turned her face away, not wanting to admire how handsome he was. She ignored the flutter of attraction in her belly.

Her eyes encountered Mrs. Jenkins' shrewd gaze and she couldn't prevent her mouth from returning the old lady's crooked smile.

Chapter Six

Katie needed to extricate herself from the awkward encounter but wasn't sure how she would accomplish it. The doctor looked unfortunately comfortable in Mrs. Jenkins' lacy room with a cup of tea in his large hand and a plate of cookies balanced on his knee.

She had hoped to get Mrs. Jenkins' measurements done, but to do so, she would have to wait for the doctor to leave. While he obviously didn't mind the sight of the old woman in her shift, it just didn't strike Katie as seemly. She felt a sigh rising up from her toes and tried to stifle it.

She must not have been successful as Katie could feel the doctor's eyes upon her, speculating. He tossed back the rest of his tea, placed the cup on the nearest table, grabbed another cookie from the plate, and got to his feet.

"Thank you for the tea, ladies. It has been a pleasure, but I ought to be on my way. I have more patients to visit before the sun sets."

Katie felt her cheeks warm at the thought that he might be leaving to make her more comfortable. Why would the man do that? She had never experienced any man putting a woman's feelings before their own. She must be mistaken and he had caught sight of the clock and realized he ought to be going. Katie offered him a cool, polite smile as he came to shake her hand.

"It was a pleasure meeting you, Mrs. Carter. I'm certain our paths will cross again shortly."

Katie merely nodded. She couldn't say it was a pleasure, and he was probably correct. In such a small town, it was inevitable that they would meet on occasion.

He took his leave of Mrs. Jenkins and then left with only the slightest backward glance.

"You certainly know how to rid the room of an eligible gentleman," Mrs. Jenkins observed drily.

Katie hoped her face projected the innocence that she felt. "I didn't say a single word to send him on his way."

Mrs. Jenkins harrumphed. "Well you certainly didn't say a single word to make him stay, either, did you?"

Katie had to laugh but persisted in her claim of innocence. "The man is a doctor and ought to be seeing to his patients rather than dallying with us."

"He wasn't dallying. It's good for my health to be able to feast my eyes on such a fine specimen of a man."

Katie laughed again. "Why, Mrs. Jenkins, that sounded almost poetic. Are you sweet on the doctor?"

Now the older woman guffawed. "He could be my grandson."

"Hardly that, Mrs. Jenkins."

"Well I am certainly at least old enough to be the man's mother. I am most certainly not sweet on him," she protested, but then had to add, "But I cannot claim to mind the man's company." Her gaze again turned shrewd. "Which is why I cannot fathom why you wouldn't want the man to stick around. You won't do any better than him in these parts."

Katie merely offered a smile in return. "Well, then it's a good thing that I am not in any need of a man or a doctor." She then turned the subject. "Now shall we get on with our plans? Your daughter-in-law mentioned that you could use a couple of new day dresses. I must tell you that the selection at the mercantile, while limited, is of good quality. I will have no problem making you what you'd like. Did you have any particular colors in mind?"

With relief, Katie was finally able to turn the older woman's attention away from the doctor and onto the matter at hand. Without too much more difficulty she had her measurements, color selections, and style determined. Katie promised to have the dresses ready within a week.

"Are you certain you can work that fast, girl? That seems like a rather optimistic estimate."

"Oh, no, Mrs. Jenkins, I am certain to be finished by then. As you can imagine, since I'm new in town, I don't have too many contracts arranged as yet. So your order will take priority."

The older woman harrumphed again but seemed quite pleased at the thought of being anyone's priority. "You make sure you allow enough time to chase after other clients though, too, young lady."

Katie grinned. "It is kind of you to concern yourself. I will have a care. Now I must be going. It has been a pleasure, Mrs. Jenkins, but now I am off to collect Annie from school. It was her first day today."

"Well why didn't you say so? Get on with you, and take good care of that little one of yours."

Katie smiled at the woman's changeable demeanor. "Good day, Mrs. Jenkins. I will see you again soon."

She then hurried to the school, hoping she'd make it on time. She had made quick work of gathering her things and taking her leave. With only one wrong turn, she arrived at the school breathless and only a minute or two late. But it was long enough to have worried the little girl.

Katie couldn't bear the stricken look in Annie's eyes. "I am so sorry, Annie. I got turned around on my way here and had to ask for help to find the school." The little girl looked confused, and Katie offered her a twisted smile. "That's the problem with us both being new to town. I wasn't completely certain how to find you. But here we are, safe and sound. No harm done, right?"

The little girl still looked concerned but she answered Katie with a nod. Katie's heart sank a little further. It was going to be difficult to entrap the child's heart with her own. She had faced so much loss in her short life; Katie couldn't really blame her for being skeptical about her adoptive mother's intentions. Katie tried not to allow it to hurt her feelings; she was the adult in the situation after all. But she had her own losses to deal with and she couldn't help wishing they both had an easier life to deal with. With a shake of her head, she gripped her satchel of supplies she had been showing Mrs. Jenkins a little tighter and determined to overcome this little setback with her new daughter.

"So how did your first day of school go, anyway? What do you think of the teacher? Are there many children your age?"

Annie was reluctant to volunteer much information, but she did answer Katie's questions. "It was all right. Mr Jones, the teacher, seems nice enough. There are three others my age, and another boy a year older but doing the same schoolwork as us. He was late starting school."

"Do you know why?"

Annie shrugged. "I don't think they lived here before."

"So, you aren't the only new one in the class. That's good, right?"

Annie shrugged again.

"Do you like school, Annie? Are you going to be able to bear going there every day?"

They were walking slowly home, and Katie thought Annie wasn't going to answer her last questions, so long was her silence. Finally the little girl looked up at her.

"I like to learn. But I worried about you all day."

Katie's heart dropped. "Oh, honey, it's not your job to worry about me. It's my job to worry about you." She pulled the child into her side with her free arm. "You needn't be worried about anything anymore. You've got me. And even Miss Melly. It's your job to be a little girl and have fun, not to worry about the adults."

"But what if something happened to you, and you didn't show up?"

Katie kept her arm tightly around the little girl. Dropping her satchel, she crouched down to be on eye level with her.

"Annie, my dear, I cannot promise that nothing bad will ever again happen in your life, but we aren't in New York anymore. The air is clean and healthy here. I'm strong and healthy. You're young and healthy. I'm quite certain we are going to be perfectly fine here together. But you're right, since I am on my own as the adult in our relationship, I ought to make some legal arrangements for someone to care for you if something did happen to me. But I can promise you this, I will do everything in my power to make sure nothing does happen to me, all right? And I promise not to be late again for picking you up from the school."

Annie regarded her with her serious gaze for another moment before a small, sweet smile peeped out on her face and she threw her arms around Katie's neck. "All right, Katie, I will try not to worry. But I cannot promise for sure."

Katie laughed with a mixture of amusement and relief. "That's all I can ask from you, sweetheart. Now let's hurry along. I left some cookie batter ready at home so we could have freshly baked cookies while you tell me a little more about your day."

Giggling, Annie stepped out of Katie's arms and started running toward home. "Come on, Katie, there are cookies waiting for us."

With a giggle of her own, Katie grabbed up her satchel with one hand, lifted the hem of her skirt with the other, and raced after the girl. With all their laughter, neither of them were very fast, and they were a giggling, exhausted heap by the time they made it to their small house on the edge of town. Melanie was just arriving home at the same time, but rather than scold them, she merely offered them a long-suffering roll of her eyes and went into her own room, leaving them to catch their breath and bake the cookies.

෨෬

"Those were the best cookies I have ever tasted, Katie. Where did you learn to cook so good?"

Katie grinned at the girl. The back of her mind twitched with the desire to correct her grammar, but she caught herself before it left her mouth. She swallowed it down and decided to leave the girl's grammar to her teacher for now.

"My mother was a wonderful cook and baker. I'm not nearly as good as she was, but everything I know, I learned from her."

"Did your mama die, too?" the youngster asked quietly, her joy in the afternoon diminishing at the reminder of loss.

"She did. I'm an orphan, just like you."

Annie looked at her with wide eyes. "Did you get adopted from a train, too?"

"Well, maybe not JUST like you. I was a fair bit older than you when my parents died. But I was all alone in the world before I found you."

"Is that why you didn't have any children already?"

Katie's mind shifted to the impossibly small coffin as it was lowered into the ground. Her breath caught for a moment, and she nearly choked on her grief. She couldn't share that with the six-year-old. Not yet. She hoped her face didn't reveal her strain as she tried to smile at the girl.

"I've been waiting for you for quite a while."

It was the right thing to say. Annie grinned at her, allowing her sorrows to recede into the background once more. Katie wished she had the resilience of a child. She had to shove her feelings aside with force. She didn't want them to worry the child.

Blinking rapidly to ensure no tears were gathering in her eyes, Katie turned away for a moment but then quickly turned back to face Annie. "Did the teacher give you any assignments you need to work on at home or would you like to help me make our supper?"

"Only the big kids get home assignments," she said with a face Katie couldn't interpret.

"Are you jealous that you didn't get one or relieved? I can't really tell."

"I think it would be way more interesting to be a big kid," Annie explained slowly. "But I don't think I would like to do school work at home."

Katie smiled. "Don't worry — you'll be a big kid soon enough. You're already six. Before you know it, you'll be all grown up. You should enjoy each day as it comes."

Annie looked at her for a moment as though she thought she had lost her mind, but then she must have seen some reason in Katie's words. She nodded. "Well, any day that comes with warm cookies is a day to be enjoyed, I'd say."

The two shared a smile before Katie started bustling about preparing the supper. Annie set the table for three and chattered away telling Katie all about the friends she had made and what she thought of her new teacher.

"In New York, I didn't get to go to school until they made me go to the orphanage. I think this school is better than that one. So I think I'll go back tomorrow."

Katie smiled. She hadn't realized that was in question. "I'm glad it's not a drudgery for you."

"What's drudgery?"

"It's hard, dull work."

Annie scrunched up her nose. "Maybe it is drudgery," she decided. "But the people are interesting."

Katie stifled the desire to laugh at the child's observations. "Were any of the other students children we met on the train?"

"Walter and Ross are in my class. They were on the train with us. I think they are very smart. Do you think it's because they're boys?"

Katie almost choked. "Are you asking me if I think they are smart because they're boys?"

Annie nodded, her eyes wide and serious.

"Most definitely not." Katie could hear the indignation in her voice and tried to quell her instinctive reactions. "I think they are a bit older than you, aren't they? That would account for them seeming smart to you. They have had more opportunity to learn things. I have every expectation that you will be as smart as or even smarter than them."

Now Annie's eyes were as wide as saucers. "Now you're telling tales, Katie. I can't be smarter than them."

"Why ever not?"

"'Cuz I'm dense."

Katie blinked at the child. "I beg your pardon."

"I'm dense. That's what the ladies at the orphanage told me. It means I'm not very smart, right?"

"I am certain that you must have mistook their meaning," Katie said while gritting her teeth to prevent herself from telling the child what she thought of any adult who would even consider saying such a thing to a child. "Never mind about them anyway. You are making a fresh start here with me, and there is every reason to believe you are going to grow up to be as successful and intelligent as you could possibly wish." She took a deep breath and switched the subject. "Now, tell me a little bit more about the game you played at recess."

The rest of the supper preparations continued without incident, and before long they were cleaning up from the meal and Katie was tucking the child into her bed.

Her heart swelled with the feeling of the small little arms around her neck as Annie told her good night.

"Sweet dreams, my dear," Katie whispered around the lump in her throat before closing the door.

She turned around to encounter Melanie's shrewd gaze upon her.

"All sorts of perils for you to navigate around as you get to know that child, aren't there?"

Katie offered a wry grin and a shuddering breath. "So many," she agreed wholeheartedly.

"Are you going to tell her about Lacey and Jason?"

"Eventually, I will. But I need her to feel secure first. If I tell her about my own losses, it will make her feel as though I do not have any power to keep her safe. She needs to see me as an authority and a source of strength for her. If she knows about my past, that will be harder for her."

Melanie's eyes filled with sympathy, but Katie tried to ignore it. Sympathy would only make her heartache swell. She needed it to be squashed down and ignored. She needed to be strong, fierce even. Nothing was going to stand in her way of making a success here, on her own, far from New York and the shadows she had left behind. She looked around her tidy little kitchen and the friend sitting at the table with her wise eyes trained upon her and grinned. She wasn't actually alone. And she was already succeeding.

"I got Mrs. Jenkins' measurements and fabric choices today. We can get started right away."

"That's wonderful. Thank you for doing that. Let's get started in the morning, though. I don't know what it is about all this clean air out here. One would think it would be invigorating, but I find that I am so sleepy."

Katie laughed. "Perhaps it is so invigorating that you wore yourself out."

"Or perhaps it was listening to your little one's prattle of her long day that wore me out," Mel countered. "I am delighted for her that she is adjusting so well to all the changes in her little life."

Katie nodded. "It's amazing how resilient a child can be." She surprised herself with a wide yawn, and they both had to smother their laughter so as not to disturb Annie.

"All right, you had the right of it. Tomorrow is soon enough to start on Mrs. Jenkins' order."

Chapter Seven

K atie and Mel made short work of Mrs. Jenkins' dresses and delivered them when Katie had predicted to the amazed delight of the older woman. She was so pleased with their work that she promised to tell everyone she encountered about their abilities. True to her word, they soon had almost as much work as they could handle. They were relieved and delighted. Their life soon settled into a comfortable routine.

Annie was chattering away as usual as Katie walked with her to school. It crossed Katie's mind that she seemed to be the only mother walking her child to school. But she so enjoyed those moments with her new daughter that she had no desire to curtail them. Besides, she hadn't been gone from New York long enough to be over the fear of all the things that could happen to a small girl on her own. Katie was certain it would be several years before she would allow the girl to go anywhere on her own. She was grateful for the circumstances that allowed her to make the short journey.

"Do you think I could?" Annie concluded.

Katie blinked. "I'm sorry, honey, I think my mind got clouded there for a moment. I didn't catch everything you said."

Annie turned her puzzled gaze up to Katie's. "But you always listen, don't you?"

"I thought so," Katie smiled. "But could you please repeat yourself?"

Annie frowned but did as she was bade. "I was telling you that Suzie wants me to play at her house on Saturday."

Katie smiled. "That sounds like it would be fun. Do you want to go?"

"I think I do."

Katie heard the uncertainty in the child's voice and wondered why this hadn't come up the evening before. "Is there a reason why you might not want to go?"

"Suzie's grandmother died. What if there's a sickness in their house?"

Katie's heart lurched for the poor child's fears. "Oh, my dear, it is sad that Suzie's grandmother died, but from what I understand, she was a really old woman. It's not unusual for people to die when they are very old. And that isn't something you can catch." She paused, allowing the child to absorb that logic. "Does Suzie seem sick to you?"

Annie shook her head. "No, I've never heard her cough, and her skin is quite pink, really."

It hurt Katie's heart that the child knew what signs to look for to sense someone's health. She offered the girl a soft smile and squeezed her hand. "You don't have to go if you don't feel comfortable, but if you would like to go, I'd be happy to take you there on Saturday. Since you don't have any brothers or sisters, it would be good for you to play with other children from time to time."

The little girl gazed at her with serious eyes. She nodded slightly. "I will think about it a little longer. But I think I'll go. It would probably be fun."

She still sounded uncertain. Katie just squeezed her hand again but decided to turn the subject. She had no intention of forcing the child.

"I have a new client to visit today. I do hope my sense of direction is improving." She laughed. "That is one of the few things I miss about New York. Since addresses were so clearly marked, it was easy to find where you were going."

The small child agreed with a sage nod before finding something new to worry about. "But you wouldn't want to move back there, would you?"

"I don't think so. I am fairly certain you and I will be quite happy here. But if I ever do find myself hankering to return, I will be sure to discuss it with you — have no fear. You and I are a team now. Where

I go, you will go, so I wouldn't make a decision like that without you agreeing to it."

"Really?"

"Truly," Katie replied with a firm nod. "Now promise me that you will try to have a marvelous day."

Annie grinned. "I promise!"

Katie watched the little girl scamper off to join a cluster of children entering the school. Her heart felt like it turned over in her chest. Having a child to love was the deepest joy, and she was eternally grateful for Annie's presence in her life. She only wished she could bear the child's concerns on her behalf. It wasn't right for a six-year-old to have so many worries. Katie hoped she would be able to restore the child's sense of security with time.

As Katie walked to her new client's home, she encountered various townspeople. It was very different than in New York. There, you would barely acknowledge other people's existence on the sidewalk, merely attempting to stay out of other people's way. Here, one must return nods and greetings, stopping to meet and exchange a few words with anyone she hadn't met before. It was the expected thing to do here, and Katie was coming to learn it was also good for business. Whenever people found out she and Melanie were seamstresses for hire other women's eyes would light up and whichever gown she was wearing would be scrutinized. Katie had taken to wearing her best examples of their workmanship whenever she left her house.

It was not in her nature to be an extrovert. Not to say that she minded the sociability of the other townspeople, but she had to struggle with her instinctive reaction to distrust those she met. She wondered if the lessons learned from her husband's hand would ever leave her.

"Good day," she nodded to another new face.

"Ma'am," the rough looking man lifted his hat and offered her a smile that appeared genuine despite the lack of a few teeth. The middle-aged woman at his side appeared delighted to encounter Katie.

"Are you the new sewing lady I've heard tell of?"

Katie contained her amusement and nodded. "Most likely," she smiled kindly. "My name is Katie Carter. My friend, Miss Melanie, and I work together on most of the sewing projects we are hired to do."

The woman clasped her hands to her chest with barely contained rapture. "Mr. Smith, this is the lady I was telling you about. Do say I can hire her. My stitches aren't nearly so fine as hers. It would be beyond wonderful to have a new going-to-church dress."

The gentleman looked slightly less pleased to meet Katie than he had originally, most likely at the thought of having to part with some of his coins, but he patted his wife's hand anyway. "Sure, sure, we'll see what we can do."

Katie didn't press the matter. "It would be a pleasure, ma'am. I am certain we will meet again. Whenever you're ready, we can make arrangements."

Much to Katie's surprise, she encountered Cassandra just coming out of the mercantile. They had arrived together on the train accompanying the orphans but had each been swept up in their own activities since soon after arriving in Bucklin.

"Katie, what a pleasure to see you!" Cassie exclaimed as she swept her into a tight hug.

Katie was amazed at the display of affection from the previously reserved young woman. She was unused to such actions from anyone but returned the woman's squeeze.

"You must accompany me to the hotel dining room for a cup of tea and fill me in on what has become of you and Mel of late. I have been so tied up with my own affairs that I haven't been much of a friend to either of you."

"Well," Katie answered reasonably, "you have certainly had many things going on."

Cassie waved her hand. "That is insufficient excuse. Do say you'll come."

After glancing at the small time piece in her reticule, Katie grinned and nodded. "I have a few moments. You are right, it would be lovely to share some tea and catch up."

Cassandra made short work of ordering for them after they had been shown to a table by the window in the starkly furnished, but still inviting, dining room.

"It is surprising how nice this room is despite the décor," Cassie commented.

"I think it's all the windows. And the smell of baking bread," Katie added with a smile. "Any room that smells like freshly baked bread is one that makes you want to linger."

Cassie nodded and grinned. She quickly brought Katie up to date on her news in a few sentences before demanding, "Now you share. Mrs. Parker told me you have taken the last child. I was so caught up with my boys on the train that I didn't get to know little Annie very much at all. Tell me everything."

Katie smiled again at the younger woman's enthusiasm. As far as she knew, there weren't too many years between them in age, but life had beaten a little of the zest out of her. Being with Cassandra reminded her of how she used to be.

"I'm not sure if I can tell you EVERYTHING. I probably don't even know all there is to know about the little darling. But she is a dear. I find it difficult to believe she was the last child remaining."

Cassie nodded and shrugged. "Most of the families wanted boys or older girls so they'd be more able to work."

Katie wrinkled her nose. "Doesn't that feel a little bit more like exploitation than adoption?"

"Don't think too hard about it or you'll break your heart. Just know that I did visit every single one of the children from our shipment, and they are all being reasonably well cared for."

"Thank you for that. You're right. I went to work at the orphanage to try to heal from my own heartbreak, but all those abandoned children just made it ache a little bit more. But I'm grateful that you checked on them. I wouldn't have had the courage."

Cassie shrugged again. "I didn't trust that the agent was going to do much. But we got lucky. This town seems to be overflowing with decent people. I don't think every single one of the children has ended up in utopian circumstances, but none of them are being mistreated."

Katie sighed. "That's better than what they had on the streets of New York, so I will try to be satisfied with that." She paused and smiled at the waiter who brought their tea and biscuits. After he left, she continued, "As for my little Annie, she is just turned six. Her entire family died from the flu that took so many last year."

"Including your family — that's something that you share," Cassie added softly. "Does she find that a comfort?"

"I haven't told her yet," Katie answered, shifting her gaze to the window before girding her courage and facing her friend. "I'm trying to inspire confidence in the child. If she knows about my losses, it might add to her fears."

Cassie didn't push the matter, for which Katie was grateful, but the compassion in her face made Katie have to swallow the lump forming in her throat. She coughed lightly to clear it and carried on briskly. "Anyhow, she's a bright little girl, quick to learn, and responds well to any guidance from me. For the most part, she seems to be taking her change of circumstances in stride, but she has a heightened fear of death. She is afraid of the doctor, and worries about going to her friend's house because the girl's grandmother died recently." She paused to sip her tea. Katie then continued in an even softer voice. "I fear I'm not going to be enough for her as a single woman. I won't be able to provide siblings for her. And I worry that every child needs the influence of both a man and a woman in their lives."

Cassie reached across the table and patted her friend's hand. "I know there's enough love in your heart to fill all the spaces this child needs. You will be enough for her — I am certain of it." There was a pause before she continued. "Of course, in a town like this, there's no shortage of potential mates for a single woman like yourself."

Katie felt that color leach from her face. "I have less than no interest in remarrying, Cassie. I am happy for you that you seem to have found a good man that makes you happy, but I am unwilling to take that chance myself. Once was quite enough for me to learn my lesson."

"Most men are not like he was," Cassandra countered quietly.

"But you never really know someone until you live with them." Katie's voice trailed off before she rallied and carried on briskly. "Anyhow, as you said, my heart definitely has plenty of room for my dear sweet Annie, and I will do all in my power to make a good life for her. Mel and I have already found a comfortable number of customers to sew for, and it provides me enough flexibility to be there for Annie. I walk with her to school and collect her after class. I visit customers while she is at school, so thus far there haven't been any conflicts. Of course, it hasn't been too long yet. I am sure there will be challenges. But so far so good."

Cassie squeezed her hand again and refrained from arguing. "I'm sure you'll make a huge success of both your sewing and being a mother." Cassie paused again. When she carried on, her tone was apologetic, as though she regretted her question even as she asked it. "Are you disappointed the teaching position fell through? You would have been able to be with her all day if you were at the school."

Katie smiled at her friend to let her know she had taken no offense from the question. "Not at all. I think it has all worked out for the best. In hindsight, it might have been too much for me to take on a large classroom of children from varying ages and backgrounds. There are currently only two classes at the school, so each teacher has children from a span of five years. I am quite content with my one little girl. And this way, I can assist her learning without being responsible for all of it." Now she turned an impish grin on her friend. "And what about you? How are you managing with your three boys on a permanent basis? Have your parents forgiven you yet?"

Cassie laughed. "Well, I never aspired to be a teacher, so I am delighted when the little darlings head off to school. It's all I can manage to keep up with their questions at the end of the day." She laughed again then sighed with contentment. "But I wouldn't have it any other way. As for my parents, I'm not completely certain if they have forgiven me for not having a high society wedding, but according to my mother's most recent letter, they are considering coming out for a visit. It does help that Charles is an Emmerson, of course."

"Of course," Katie agreed with a chuckle, shaking her head over the ridiculousness of the wealthy. She was determined that her daughter would learn to fend for herself. Katie would never expect the girl to need a husband to support her. Realizing that her heart had begun to race, she took a deep breath to calm her nerves, reminding herself once again that surely not all men were dangerous.

The clock in the hallway sounded the hour. With a start, Katie realized that time was slipping by. She quickly got to her feet.

"It was so nice to have a little visit, Cass. Do stop by the house the next time you're in town, please. I'm terribly sorry to cut it short, but I really must be on my way."

"No apologies needed, my friend. Get on with your business. You were straight with me from the beginning. I promise I will come by really soon."

With a quick, tight hug, Katie said goodbye and then hurried away. She needed to reach her destination, conduct her appointment, and then return for Annie before the child became anxious. Katie's new reason to live was to ensure Annie was comfortable. It crossed her mind that this sounded obsessive, but she shoved the thought from her mind. It was a mother's obligation to see to the well being of her child, she reassured herself. Once they were settled into a routine, she would strive for balance. But in the meantime, it wouldn't harm either of them if she obsessed a little over her new daughter's happiness. After the losses they both had endured, it was just what they both needed.

Katie was relieved that her new client knew exactly what she wanted and was ready for her when she arrived. The style the woman was asking for, while a little more complicated than what she and Melanie usually did, wasn't beyond their abilities.

"It might take a day or two extra, though, to make sure all the pleating and embroidery is just so," Katie cautioned the woman.

"That's all right," Mrs. Levitt assured her. "I've been waiting for years for someone to say they could make me my dream dress. I can easily wait a couple extra days."

Katie was relieved by the woman's easygoing reaction and reminded herself once more that her decision to settle in Bucklin had been a wise one.

She was nearly skipping with contentment as she made her way back toward the school. Her bouncing steps came to a swift, stuttering halt when she recognized who was striding toward her. She glanced around quickly for an avenue of escape. One more thing to miss from New York. There were always alleys one could scurry down in the big city. Here in this town, it would be far too embarrassingly obvious if she tried to avoid him.

"Good afternoon, Mrs. Carter. What a pleasure to run into you on this fine day." Dr. Jeffries lifted his hat to her. She tried not to find it gallant. She averted her eyes so that her gaze wouldn't be drawn by his handsome features. Katie would not allow them to dwell on his sharp cheekbones or warm green eyes. And she most certainly would not glance at the charming dimple that was sure to peep at her if he smiled. The cookie Mrs. Levitt had offered her began to revolve uncomfortably in her stomach.

Katie realized she hadn't responded but was merely standing still staring off into the distance like a simpleton. With a disgusted roll of her eyes, she offered the doctor a slight curtsy.

"Good afternoon, sir. I cannot tarry as I have to collect my daughter from the school."

"Of course, I would never wish to detain you." He offered her a slight bow.

Katie could feel hot color splashing high on her cheeks, but she avoided meeting the doctor's gaze as she hurried past him. She knew it was ridiculous. He was probably a decent man. She had never heard any of the townsfolk speak anything but well of him.

She felt like a fool. And well she should, she assured herself harshly. It was foolish to be afraid of a man just because he was handsome. Surely not all handsome men were cruel and dangerous. Most would consider his good looks an asset. Katie had even heard some of the women giggling about what good medicine it was to look at the doctor. But she couldn't agree.

Chapter Eight

K atie strolled along, content to enjoy the music in the air. The leaves rustling, the birds chirping, the crunch of the gravel under her feet. It was nothing like the city. And she loved it. For the first time in years she felt contentment. It had taken her a while to figure out what the sensation was. Then she realized that for the first time in maybe her entire life, she wasn't consumed with worries or anxieties. Sure, she was concerned for her and Annie's future, but she was filled with confidence that she was up to the task of facing it. Despite the abuse she had faced at her husband's hands and words, she had fought hard to regain her sense of self. She now knew what it meant to be happy. And she would do whatever it took to maintain that for herself and her daughter.

She felt like skipping but thought it would be too undignified for a matron like herself. She grinned. Maybe once Annie was with her. She picked up her pace, eager to see Annie after the afternoon's absence. She laughed out loud before glancing around quickly. Even though she wasn't in a city anymore, there were still people around and she didn't want anyone thinking she was crazy. She grinned. What did it matter? No one's opinion mattered but her own. She laughed again. She felt as though she were glowing from the joy in her heart.

When she arrived at her destination, she couldn't find anyone at first. The house appeared to be empty. No one responded to her increasingly fervent knocking. Her worry escalated. She ran around to the back of the house. It felt as though her heart was lodged in her throat when she saw the group clustered behind the barn. She couldn't see clearly through the tangle of legs, but lying on the ground was a bright splash of color that exactly matched the frock Annie had worn that morning to go play with her friend.

Katie shoved her fist into her mouth to stifle the scream that was trying to escape her throat. Picking up her skirts, she ran over to the group. Suzie's mother grabbed her before she got all the way to her daughter. At the moment, in her mounting fear, Katie couldn't remember the family name and wasn't about to tax her brain with figuring it out.

"Mrs. Carter, dear, you can't be letting your wee one see you in a taking. We've called for the doctor, he should be here any moment. Take a deep breath now." The older woman had spoken in a low, soothing voice but right by her ear, so Katie heard her clearly. She knew she needed to calm down and the woman had meant well, but the thought of the doctor coming for her daughter had her in a worse state than seeing her on the ground had. She knew that no one called the doctor unless it was absolutely necessary. Most farmers had the basic skills needed to patch up the usual scrapes and bruises children accumulated.

Closing her eyes, Katie willed strength into her limbs. *You've been through worse, Katie girl, you can handle this. Nothing will happen to Annie. Breathe.* She listened to her inner voice and took a deep steadying breath before pulling her arm out of the other woman's grasp with a small smile to let her know she meant no offense. The crowd parted, and she was by her daughter's side, dropping to her knees and hovering to ascertain the damage.

"What happened?" she asked, proud to hear that her voice sounded reasonably steady.

"The girls thought they would try flying," Suzie's father answered wryly with a gesture toward the opening above their heads. Katie could see it was a well stocked haymow. Her eyes widened as she looked back down at her daughter.

"Is your daughter all right?"

"She lost her nerve and didn't jump. She climbed down and came for help when your little one got hurt. I'm right sorry, Mrs. Carter. I know your girl is from the city. Ours should've known better and stopped her."

Katie appreciated the man's words, but despite her devastation, she couldn't let the other little girl take the full blame. "I would have thought Annie would have the sense to know jumping from such a height is a bad idea. But never mind about that now. Has she been moved? Can I touch her? Is she bleeding anywhere?"

"I will ascertain that for you right now," came a deep voice from behind her. Katie stifled her involuntary reaction. For a moment, she wanted to throw herself into the doctor's arms. But that would be wrong on so many levels. Most of all because he was there to tend to her child, not soothe her rattled nerves. She offered him a tight smile by way of greeting.

"Thank you, doctor."

He didn't return her smile, keeping his full focus on Annie. Katie didn't mind; it was where it should be. She could barely breathe; her chest was so tight with anxiety. She reminded herself once more to keep the air flowing into her lungs. The last thing any of them needed was for her to collapse next to her daughter.

The doctor made short work of examining the child. He worked swiftly but before he could even finish, Annie coughed and slowly opened her eyes. When what she saw was the doctor, she screamed her alarm and burst into tears. Katie quickly pushed the doctor aside and gathered her daughter into her arms.

"Oh, my poor darling, everything is going to be fine. Tell me where it hurts." Katie tried to be soothing.

"Am I dying? I don't want the doctor. I told you I shouldn't have come here." Her words came out in jerking gasps around her sobs.

"Hush now, Annie. You most certainly are not dying. But you did a very foolish thing when you jumped out of that window, and this is the consequence. You need to let the doctor finish checking to make sure you didn't do any serious damage to yourself."

"No, please, no doctor," Annie whimpered.

Katie forced herself to meet Doctor Jeffries' gaze. "Were you finished with your examination?"

"I still need to examine her head," he answered quietly.

Annie burrowed closer into Katie's arms. "Shhh, darling, it will all be fine. How about if I hold onto you, and he just feels around to make sure you didn't crack it like an egg?"

Her pitiful attempts at levity actually had an effect. Annie's sobs were interrupted, and a watery chuckle emerged from the child. "I'm not an egg."

"No, and you're not a bird either, as you have learned the hard way, didn't you?" she reminded the child quietly. "Now just cuddle right into me, my dear, and I'm sure Mr. Jeffries will be as quick as he can." She offered the doctor a pointed look when she mentioned speed, hoping he wouldn't take offense over her lack of his medical title. Katie felt there was no need to remind the child she was being examined by the dreaded doctor.

He must have understood her meaning since he offered her a small wink before he continued with his gentle examination.

"I am quite sure she only knocked the wind out of herself with a rough landing, but this lump on her head does give me some concern. The fact that she hasn't vomited is reassuring, but you will have to watch her closely for the next day or two. Will that be a problem for you? If you cannot remain with her, perhaps Mrs. Marsden could keep her for you."

Katie was horrified at the suggestion. She didn't want to offend the other woman, but she could barely contain her gasp of shock. "I beg your pardon? Of course, I can manage to keep close watch over my daughter." She glared at the man, but her dirty look barely seemed to faze him. His cold stare chilled her to the bone as she clutched her now quiet daughter to her chest. She couldn't understand his sudden change of attitude. Just a moment ago, he had seemed almost comforting as he accepted her reluctance to call him doctor. She didn't think she had any composure left, but she gathered the last shreds of her dignity and, with Annie still clinging tightly, she managed to get herself to her feet. Glancing around at the gathered spectators, she offered them all a tight nod and a thinly polite smile.

"Thank you for your help," she offered vaguely to everyone and stepped away from the group, walking slowly so as not to jar her pale child.

"Are you mad at me, Mama?" Annie's quiet voice broke the silence that had surrounded them as they made their way home.

Katie's heart constricted at the sweet sound of being someone's mother. But she hurried to reassure the child. "Of course I'm not mad at you, sweetheart. You have many things you have to learn. It's unfortunate you had to learn this lesson the hard way, but I'm sure you'll never make the mistake of trying to fly ever again, will you?"

"Never, ever," the child said. Her voice was still low but her mouth was less droopy as at least one of her concerns was lessened. "The doctor seemed to be mad, though, didn't he?"

Katie sighed. "Yes, he did, but don't worry yourself too much over that. We don't need to concern ourselves with what anyone else thinks. If he didn't see fit to tell us why he was mad, then we needn't bother about it either."

"Are you very certain?"

Now Katie had to grin. "I am absolutely one hundred percent certain that I do not give a fig for that man's thoughts, as long as he has assured me that you are well, he can keep the rest of it to himself."

Despite her continued pallor, Annie grinned at Katie for a moment before more concerns came to her mind. "Am I too heavy for you to carry? Maybe you should put me down and I can walk."

Katie shook her head. "You gave me quite a fright when I saw you lying on the ground. I am finding comfort in having you in my arms. And you are not nearly heavy enough. I am starting to think that I haven't been feeding you as much as I ought."

This seemed to do the trick of turning the child's mind away from her worries as she was able to let out a small giggle and begin to imagine how she could fatten up.

"Maybe we could stop at the mercantile and buy some sweets," she suggested with a wiggle.

Katie laughed. "Or maybe we could bake a cake when we get home."

"Oh, that would be wonderful, then we can share with Miss Mel, too."

"I think that is the best idea. No doubt Miss Mel could use some extra flesh on her bones as well." Katie said that just as they were approaching their small house, her voice pitched just right so that Melanie, who was standing near the open window, could hear. She burst into laughter as she opened the door wide for them to enter.

"Might I ask why we are discussing plumping me up?" the laughter in her voice revealed that she had not taken offense.

Katie quickly explained what had happened in as light a tone as she could muster. She was relieved to see that while Melanie's brows furrowed with concern, she saved her questions for later.

The afternoon and evening passed quickly while they kept the youngster occupied with quiet activities, enjoying the quickly assembled and cooled cake before they tucked her into bed.

"Now you really must tell me why you are as pale as death. It seems to me that the child has come to no serious injury."

Katie flushed over her friend's words. "If you had seen her lying there on the ground with everyone standing around her wringing their hands, you would not be quite so complacent."

"I dare say I wouldn't, but it still seems to me that you are concerned about more than just the girl's injuries. Did something else happen today? Did something go wrong with the client you went to visit?"

Katie grinned. "No, I almost forgot about it, but the visit with Mrs. Bainbridge went very well. I think, if we please her with this first commission, we will get a good bit of business from her. The dear woman was almost beside herself with delight at the thought of someone else making her gowns and frocks. It seemed to me that while she had exceptional taste, her skills are merely middling. But since her husband seems to be doing quite well for himself, he shan't begrudge her the expense."

"Well that is excellent news. I am certain we will please her. So what else is troubling you?"

Katie chuckled, then sighed. "I do believe you have come to know me a little too well." She paused, rubbing her neck to try to release some of the tension that had accumulated there. "Annie's accident brought back a few too many unpleasant feelings. I'm sure you can relate. You never completely leave old grief behind, and new frights can bring them to the fore."

"That's certainly true." Mel's soft, accepting tone prompted Katie to continue.

She looked at Mel and felt heat creep into her cheeks. "The doctor was called before I got there."

"Oooo, the handsome, young doctor?" Mel teased.

"I do believe this town only has the one doctor."

Mel laughed. "Perhaps so, but why does his having been called cause a crease to your forehead? I know Annie has an unreasonable fear of doctors — has she infected you with her concerns?"

Katie laughed too but added a small shrug. "After seeing all the sickness and death we have seen, doctors don't usually bring warm feelings to the heart."

Mel nodded but then added reasonably, "They do occasionally bear good news, such as when they assist with a birth." Katie shot her a wry look, prompting a laugh from Mel. "Very well, I will agree that doctors are usually accompanying trouble. But since he's so very handsome, it must help assuage the problem a little bit, or at least distract you from your troubles."

"I will admit, the doctor is one of the best looking men I've ever laid eyes on, but he seems to have taken me in dislike. I don't think he approves of women who work."

Mel appeared to be taken aback by this statement. "All women work," she replied firmly.

"Well, of course, but I meant for pay, as in employment."

Mel sniffed. "Well, then you needn't wrinkle up your forehead over such a ridiculous man. If he is so backwards as that, you needn't bother considering his thoughts."

Katie chuckled. "That was exactly the conclusion I had reached myself, but I worry about how influential he might be in this size of a town."

"Never mind about him. Very few of the women, who we are hoping will be our clients, will pay him any heed if he starts spouting off about women working outside the home. Most women have the sense to realize that life is not so straightforward."

Katie agreed with her friend but still couldn't put away the worry that buzzed around the back of her mind as she settled into her bed that night. Thankfully, the fresh clean air of Bucklin and all the walking she had done that day were more powerful than her troubled thoughts, and she quickly drifted off into a deep sleep.

After waking Annie up a couple times during the night to ensure she was doing well, they all slept later than usual. But after a hearty breakfast and getting Annie settled with a small chalkboard, Katie hurried away from the small house to meet with one client nearby.

"Mrs. Carter?" Katie froze in her tracks when she heard the incredulous tone of the familiar, deep, masculine voice.

"Good morning, Dr. Jeffries," she replied, keeping her tone light, as she wondered whether or not she should just brush by him or if she ought to stay and converse with the man. The disapproval clearly displayed on his face made her feel much inclined to do the former. She was about to do just that when he interrupted her thoughts.

"I thought you said you were in a position to keep an eye on Annie for a couple of days. It hasn't even been twenty-four hours."

Katie bristled at his accusatory tone but tried to convince herself that she appreciated his concern for her daughter. "I woke her up every few hours through the night, just as you instructed, doctor. And I spent most of the morning with her. But I had to make one quick call on a neighbor today. I haven't been gone long. In the meantime, Melanie is with her."

"What was so important that it couldn't wait until you were absolutely certain your child is well?" the doctor scoffed.

"Keeping food on her table and a roof over her head, doctor." Katie bit out the words, trying, but failing, to remain polite. "Not that it's any of your business what I do with my time."

"I don't know how you convinced the ones organizing the adoptions to entrust you with a child, but it seems to me that you are unfit for the assignment."

Katie could feel the color drain from her face as she felt his insult all the way to her core. A part of her wanted to curl up in a ball in a secluded corner and wail her grief at all the injustices life had handed her. But another part of her refused to let another man speak to her in a hurtful way.

"Dr. Jeffries, you do not have any right to speak to me in such a manner. Surely a man who has sworn to care for the well being of others would be sufficiently informed to realize that a woman on her own with a child has to do whatever it takes to care for all the responsibilities. While it would, of course, be absolutely lovely if I were somehow independently wealthy and didn't have to be gainfully employed, that is not the reality I face. I need to be attentive to my clients in order to make sure that Melanie and I can have enough business to succeed. Thankfully, my business partner is a trustworthy woman who could sit with my child for the few minutes that I had to be away. I am not being derelict in my duties. And you are exceedingly foolish to have thought that I was, and unnecessarily cruel to have told me so, especially given the stress that I had to contend with yesterday and the less than restful night I dealt with last night. I pray I never require your services in the future." If she was of a calmer mind, she would be happy to see that he seemed to have been struck mute by her words, but all she wanted to do now was be somewhere else. He seemed rooted in his place so she had to prod, "Now, if you would be so kind as to get out of my way, I will no longer trouble you with my presence."

෨൫

Wyatt stepped off the path in order to allow her plenty of room to pass. He watched, dumbfounded, as she swept away from him with her head held high but her lips trembling. If he could, he would rip out his own tongue for the pain he had obviously caused her.

It was this ridiculous attraction he felt toward her that had muddled his mind, he was certain of it. He was so torn up about his feelings for the lovely young widow. A part of him wanted to sweep her into his arms and care for all her worries. But another part of him balked at the thought of taking such a headstrong woman into his life. With all that he faced each day, he was certain he required a soothing presence in his home at the end of the day. While Mrs. Carter was more than pleasant to look at, he was quite certain she had too many thoughts of her own to ever be able to soothe away his cares.

But Patricia had been a soothing presence, at least for the most part, and that didn't work out so well, his subconscious reminded him. He chose to ignore that mocking voice and hurried on to his next appointment. But before he got too far away, he couldn't resist turning back to observe the pretty brunette's progress. It troubled him to see that her head was no longer held high, and her strides were not nearly so purposeful as when she had swept away from him. It looked to him as though she had drooped.

The doctor had to fight hard to stop himself from running toward her. He fought the impulse that made him want to draw her into his arms and croon to her like a small child. She always seemed so strong; he doubted she would welcome such a gesture anyway. But she didn't look quite so strong now. He really ought to have curbed his tongue.

He resolved to speak more kindly to her the next time they encountered one another. Despite her desire to never require his services, he was most certain they would cross paths many times again in the small town.

Chapter Nine

Wyatt was quite correct in his assumptions. It was barely two days later when they were forced into one another's company once again.

He knew he was meandering, but he couldn't bring himself to hurry. Checking Mrs. Jenkins' boils was sure to be the low point of his day. He would much rather enjoy the beautiful sunshiny day and allow his mind to wander to its favorite hobby of late — daydreaming about remarrying and starting a family. It troubled him slightly that in recent days the imaginary wife had taken on the features of Mrs. Carter, but he tried to ignore her face and just enjoy the imaginary sensation of having someone to come home to at the end of the day. And the imaginary enjoyment of the delicious scent of freshly baked bread or cookies. Wyatt chuckled as he caught himself inhaling deeply, as though he really could smell the delectable aroma. Shaking his head over his own foolishness, the doctor goaded his horse into a faster pace. He really ought to get on with the dreaded task.

After tying his horse loosely in the shade of a large tree near the road, Wyatt made his way toward the house. He stopped for a moment to admire how tidy the yard was despite Mrs. Jenkins' health problems. It was one more benefit of having a wife. Even an invalid was more benefit than trouble, he thought, remembering the good times with his dearly departed.

Shaking his head again, he quickly approached the door and rapped decisively.

"Is that you, Doctor Jeffries? Please hurry and come in."

Wyatt blinked. Had his imaginings conjured the woman? That sounded like Mrs. Carter.

"Whoever it is, please come in. We need your help."

Wyatt pulled himself out of his sudden inertia and opened the door. He was unsurprised to see Mrs. Carter but was shocked to see her huddled over Mrs. Jenkins' prone form.

"What has happened?" he demanded. He had almost asked 'what have you done,' but caught himself before making such a foolish mistake. But his tone must have given away some of his thoughts because the lovely widow shot him another one of her fierce glares.

"I cannot say for certain, Doctor Jeffries, what has happened to her, but she is bleeding quite terribly, which is why I wasn't able to run for help. Thankfully, she had mentioned to me that you were to be stopping by today, so I was able to remain here without losing my mind completely. I can assure you, my daughter was in the pink of perfect health when I left her at school this morning. And Mrs. Jenkins' bleeding was not my doing. Even if I had poked the poor dear with needles while checking her hem, there shouldn't be this much blood."

She seemed to be rambling, no doubt caused by her fear, but his silence didn't seem to be reassuring her at all. Perhaps she realized she was giving too much away. Her face hardened, and she offered him another glare. "I should actually be demanding of you what has happened to her. Why did you take so long in getting here? While it feels like I have been sitting here with her for several lifetimes, it has in reality been at least half an hour. And why is she not healed already? She was suffering from her boils the first time I visited her. Surely you should have fixed her up by now, shouldn't you?"

Wyatt grinned. He hadn't been railed at by anyone in ages. He normally appreciated the respect afforded him by the townsfolk, but it was refreshing to be treated like a regular person. It was obvious to him that Mrs. Carter most certainly did not place him in any position of reverence.

The young woman was looking at him as though he had lost his mind. He realized he was just standing there grinning like a simpleton when he should really be doing something to help his patient.

"You are quite correct, Mrs. Carter, I should have gotten here sooner. I didn't realize she was in such a bad way. When I was here last time, I thought her boils were almost better. Something must have happened to make her take a turn for the worse." There was a moment of silence while Mrs. Carter absorbed his words and appeared somewhat mollified. "She's most fortunate that you were here to lend her assistance. You did very well in staunching the bleeding."

"Imagine that! You are saying the poor soul is fortunate that I was visiting a client rather than sitting at home being a housewife." The widow's sarcastic tone made heat accumulate in Wyatt's face. He offered her a wry smile.

"Well, it was fortuitous that she was not alone," he commented as he continued his assessment of the situation. "You say you have been here for half an hour, and it is still bleeding? That is very odd."

"The bleeding has slowed significantly, but whenever I would remove the towel, hoping I could go for help, it was obvious that it hadn't stopped. I was concerned she would lose all her blood if I left her."

"You did the right thing in staying with her. Thank you for remaining calm," he remarked.

She offered him a crooked smile. "I did not say I remained calm, doctor. I remained present. Most of me wanted to scream with fear. It was the first time since I arrived in Bucklin that I wished we were still in New York. In the city, all I would have had to do is shout and someone would have heard me and come to our aid. All this beautiful space can be a problem when you run into trouble and are alone."

Wyatt frowned. "That is why it is best for women not to be alone, then."

The widow laughed lightly. "Well, you certainly don't change your tune, do you?" Without allowing time for him to explain himself, she continued, "Now tell me what I can do to assist you. While a part of me wants to run out of here as quickly as my feet can carry me now that you are here to take care of her, I cannot bear to see the poor dear so pale. Surely there is something to be done."

Wyatt blinked, brought back to the task at hand. He was being daft, staring at the lovely young widow and forgetting about the poor woman on the floor. He focused his mind and started issuing orders as clearly as possible.

"We will need lots of warm water and as many towels as you can find. If there is not enough water in the house, one of us will have to go out to the well. Poor Mrs. Jenkins doesn't have running water in the house. If you'd like to stay with her, I can go fetch a couple pails of water."

"No!" she declared before blushing charmingly. She lowered her voice. "I am ashamed to admit, I cannot bear the thought of being alone here with her again feeling so helpless. I can manage the water. You stay with your patient." Her flush deepened while she paused before adding, "But I thank you for the offer. I'm sure you meant to be chivalrous, but I am quite capable despite being squeamish."

Wyatt had to laugh despite the seriousness of their situation. The defensive woman was cute when she got flustered. He realized she resented his implication that she was less capable than he was, but she also resented her own weakness in admitting how afraid she had been while alone with the bleeding older woman. He ought to tell her how impressed he was with her presence of mind, but she was likely to consider his words to be condescension. Besides, she was already out the door. At least she wasn't standing around wringing her hands. As much as he might think women ought to be tending to the home and the children rather than trying to be employed, he had to admit that Mrs. Carter was being quite sensible in this difficult situation. If he had been here by himself with Mrs. Jenkins, he would be almost as stuck as Mrs. Carter had been, despite his tools and training. Sometimes more than one pair of hands was necessary. That thought could be quite distracting in the context of thinking of the lovely widow, so he shoved it from his mind.

ഇ൦ൽ

The bucket made a loud splash as it hit the surface of the water. Katie gritted her teeth as she turned the winch that would pull the full bucket back up. She had been a little too full of bravado when she told the doctor that it would be no problem to fetch the water. But she would rather do it than stay with poor Mrs. Jenkins on her own. It was too bad, though, that no one had told her how to get the bucket to be only half full. Maybe if she had been faster. Katie sighed and tugged on the handle. There was no question that she would sleep like a log tonight after the fright she had and now the exertion. With a great deal of effort and more grunting than she would like to admit, she finally had two pails full of water. She carefully lifted them, desperately trying not to spill a single drop after all the effort it took to collect. Going as quickly as she could while balancing the buckets gingerly, Katie returned to the house in time to see Mrs. Jenkins regain consciousness.

"Oh, my dear girl, I am so sorry for the trouble I've caused you. Look at your face, all red from fetching the water. You should have let the doctor do it, dear."

Katie laughed. "I am so glad to see you awake, Mrs. Jenkins. I'm sorry to admit to you that I had no wish to remain with you by myself in this house for another minute. When Dr. Jeffries gave me the choice of fetching the water or staying with you, I chose the lesser of two evils. I was terrified when you fainted on me earlier."

The older woman chuckled and then winced when the doctor prodded her wound. "You are a good girl, Katie. I am grateful you were here."

Katie grinned back at her client. "Despite the fright you gave me, I'm glad I was here, too. But I'm even more glad that the doctor finally arrived." Katie set the buckets down carefully in the kitchen before ladling some of the water into a large kettle to boil. Once she was satisfied that it would soon be ready, she hurried to the closet where she had seen Mrs. Jenkins stored her towels. With an armful of towels, she turned back toward the other occupants of the room and almost dropped them all when she realized they were both watching her like a curious specimen.

"What is it? Do I have smut on my face?" She was embarrassed and didn't pause to wait for a reply. "You know, I'm not very used to using a well like that. It was more work than I expected because I didn't really know what I was doing. But I managed to get quite a bit of water, which should be almost boiled by now."

She could feel the heat as it climbed high onto her cheekbones, but she tried to ignore her embarrassment as the other two exchanged amused glances. Katie didn't want to be rude to her customer, but a part of her desperately wanted to stick her tongue out at the two of them. Ignoring them, she turned away to check on the water after carefully placing the bundle of towels near the doctor's left hand.

"She's such a good girl, wouldn't you agree, doctor?"

"I would, Mrs. Jenkins. You would be in a bad way if she hadn't been with you when you started to bleed."

Katie's embarrassment mounted as she listened to them discuss her.

"And she's such a pretty little thing, too," Mrs. Jenkins continued. Katie could just imagine the devilish twinkle in her eye as she said that, but she kept her hot face turned away and tried to focus on her task of getting the water to boil. She doubted if watching the pot would make it boil faster but maybe the heat from her face would help, she thought with a wry twist of her lips. Involuntarily, her ears strained to hear the doctor's response.

"She's so little, I would think that a good stiff breeze might blow her away, but she did manage to bring in two heavy buckets of water for us, so there's a fair bit of might packed into the little package." The doctor had kept his voice low, but Katie still heard him and was touched by his words. She prided herself on her independence. It had been such a fight for her to regain confidence in herself after the treatment she had endured under her husband's hands. She was a little disgusted with herself for the fact that hearing a man voice a positive comment about her felt so good to her heart.

Despite her watching it, the kettle finally began to boil, and she couldn't dither any longer. She poured some of the boiling water into a pot half full of the cooler water from outside and carried it back toward the patient.

"I think this is a good temperature. If you'll check it, I can add more boiled water or more cool, if you think it needs adjusting." She was trying not to babble, but it was a challenge with the handsome doctor's gaze on her.

He reached out and touched the pot. "It is perfect. Thank you, Mrs. Carter."

Katie kept her head down in an effort to hide her heightened color and to avoid Mrs. Jenkins' knowing gaze. But she couldn't get away from the older lady's delighted chuckle.

The next few minutes passed in near silence as she worked in remarkable harmony with the doctor. Despite her antipathy toward him, they were able to cooperate quite well, as though they had experience working together. No doubt her experience nursing her family as they were sick and dying gave her a skilled perspective to the task at hand.

They soon had Mrs. Jenkins patched up and settled onto a comfortable chair with her feet propped up and a cup of tea within reach.

"I'm sorry, Katie dear, that you had to take so much time with me today, and we still didn't get our business concluded. At this point, I'm just not up to it now."

"Of course not, Mrs. Jenkins, please don't trouble yourself over it at all. I am glad that I was here when you needed someone, and I'll be happy to come back in a few days to check on you. If you're up for it then we can proceed, otherwise, I will return again another time."

"You are a dear, thank you."

Katie grinned. Even though the older woman was a bit crotchety at times, Katie was becoming quite fond of her. And she was amused and delighted to find that the cranky woman had decided to approve of her. She was a firm believer in a woman's need for friends, and she would be proud to count Mrs. Jenkins among her own small circle.

The doctor was quickly packing up his things as Katie was taking her leave. "If you'll wait a moment, I'll walk you out," he said to her. Katie wanted to refuse but didn't want to do so in front of Mrs. Jenkins. She offered him a tight smile but didn't say anything. With her own small bag of supplies looped over her arm, she waited by the door with something slightly less than patience as he said his goodbyes.

"I will stop in on you tomorrow, Mrs. Jenkins. See that you move as little as possible so you don't reopen your wound. You should have one of your daughters-in-law or granddaughters come in to help you for a few days. You do too much. You really need to get these all healed properly, and it seems to me that only bed rest will do the trick."

Mrs. Jenkins grumbled a bit about this but finally agreed to ask for help. Katie couldn't help but smile about her cantankerous attitude, and so she wasn't frowning when the doctor finally joined her.

They walked out of the house and toward the doctor's horse in silence. She didn't have anything to say to him. She didn't appreciate his vacillating attitude toward her and her need to support herself and her daughter. But she didn't want to antagonize him any more than she already had. And she hadn't hated working with him this afternoon, either. She sighed.

"I must thank you again for your assistance today, Mrs. Carter." The doctor's voice sounded stiff, as though he were reluctant to utter the words.

Katie laughed. "You don't have to do that, doctor. It seems to be a chore for you. And I didn't mind at all. Mrs. Jenkins is a dear, and I was glad to help her."

"Well, I would have been hard pressed to look after her so well if I had been there on my own," Doctor Jeffries insisted.

Katie laughed again. "That is true, doctor. I cannot even tell you how terrified I was when I was there on my own. I doubt you would have been scared, as you have the knowledge and experience that I lack, but there is only so much that can be done with two hands."

She didn't know how to interpret the expression on his face. It was as though he didn't know what to do with her. She could relate. Her feelings toward him were such a jumble. She didn't want to be near him but tended to enjoy herself when she was with him, so long as he wasn't commenting on her need for employment. She felt like laughing again but didn't want him to think she was a lunatic.

"I ought to be going. Melanie will be worrying about me."

"And well she should. You really shouldn't be roaming around on your own like you do."

Katie laughed, with a little less amusement this time. "And there we go, back to where we started, despite how well we were doing this afternoon." Her tone was dry. He looked as though he was going to interject, but she didn't allow him to. "I'm glad I was there to help. Thank you for rescuing me and poor Mrs. Jenkins this afternoon. I will wish you a good day."

Without waiting for him to respond she hurried away.

&ps;ॐ&cq;

Wyatt watched her go. He just stood there and watched her brisk strides as she got on with her own affairs. He didn't say anything to stop her. He didn't grab her arm. He did none of the things that were rushing through his mind to keep her by his side. A part of him was disappointed to see her go. The other part was wondering where he had left his mind because it seemed to be lost.

You want a mild-mannered, lady-like woman to stay at home, look after your babies, and have your house smelling like freshly baked cookies when you come home, he reminded himself. *Yes, Mrs. Carter is a pleasure to look at and was amazingly helpful today, but she is not the one for you, so keep your eyes to yourself.*

Despite his lecture to himself, he remained standing there watching her retreating form until she disappeared into the copse of trees that separated the Jenkins' property from its neighbors.

When he could no longer see her, he glanced around sheepishly, hoping Mrs. Jenkins hadn't seen him mooning around like a love-struck teenager. She would be sure to let him know what she thought of him on the morrow. He felt his lips twist into a wry smile. He surely was losing his mind.

His wife had been a sweet, gentle soul when he had met her when they were children. Her illness had confined her to the house, and she had kept herself occupied with books. The more she learned, the more opinionated she had become. While Mrs. Carter's healthy vitality was beyond attractive, her fierce independence and strong opinions had a tendency to irritate him beyond reason.

ᏚᎾᏨ

"Why are you still single, Doctor Jeffries? Did you never want a wife? I saw you watching Mrs. Carter yesterday. You cannot tell me you are indifferent to her."

He tried not to flinch over the questions as he examined Mrs. Jenkins' wound.

"I was married. I am a widower."

His bald words won him a moment of silence, but she soon rallied. "Really, doctor?" the fascination in her tone informed him he wouldn't be getting away without telling her at least some of his story. "What happened to the poor dear soul? She must've been awfully young to die. Was it childbirth?"

Wyatt stifled his exasperated sigh. Her questions were rude, but her curiosity was probably justifiable. The poor old woman was bored and hating her confinement.

"No, it wasn't childbirth. My wife had a wasting disease. We never could get a final, proper diagnosis. It is why I became a doctor, actually."

"Has she been gone long, dear?"

The sympathy he could hear in her voice brought a lump to his throat that he had to clear before he could answer her. "It was before

I moved to Bucklin, of course. She has been gone three and a half years."

"You must have loved her very much if you have remained single this long."

Wyatt forced a grin. "I came out here not long after we buried her. And if you haven't noticed, eligible young woman are rather rare in these parts."

"Not so much anymore," Mrs. Jenkins argued, her tone sly. "The train with all them orphans brought some women with it, from what I've heard. Isn't Mrs. Carter one of those ladies?"

Wyatt hoped his face didn't betray his embarrassment. "I do believe you're right, Mrs. Jenkins. Perhaps I will get a chance to meet some of them."

"Well, you've more than met one of them. You can't tell me you didn't enjoy Mrs. Carter's company yesterday. I saw you watching her walk away. You certainly didn't look indifferent to me."

Wyatt sighed. "It's complicated, Mrs. Jenkins."

She snorted. "What is that supposed to mean?"

He couldn't help laughing over her question. His examination was finished. He wanted to run away, but looking after the old lady's mental health was part of his care for her. Appeasing her curiosity would probably help her stay off her feet.

Pulling a chair closer to the older woman, Wyatt made himself comfortable. He had a feeling he would be here for a while. Before the silence could stretch into discomfort, he finally started to explain himself.

"Mrs. Carter seems to be a pleasant young woman, but I think I would prefer a wife with a little less fire in her."

Mrs. Jenkins raised her eyebrows at him. "Seems to me, her fire is half her appeal."

Wyatt chuckled. He couldn't really argue with her observation.

"And if you have a mind to remain in Bucklin, a mousey woman might not make it," she pointed out.

"I didn't say I want a mousey woman," he protested.

"You can't have it both ways, doctor." She eyed him speculatively. "What was your dearly departed like?"

"We grew up together. She was my best friend. When we were children, she could climb a tree almost as fast as me. And then she got sick. We got married before we realized quite how ill she really was. I did everything I could think of to get her well. But nothing worked."

"Did her sickness affect her personality?" Her shrewd question made him wish he had never allowed this conversation to continue. He couldn't answer her question. She took his silence as affirmation. "Don't judge a strong woman by the same standard as a cantankerous sick lady. They are not one and the same — I'm sure you realize that."

Wyatt could feel himself sputtering. "Well, of course I know that."

When she just gazed at him, he felt his face growing warm and he sighed. "My head knows that, Mrs. Jenkins. But my heart would never wish to take the chance on living like that ever again. My wife had been my best friend. But I lost her quite a while before her death. It was a painful time."

"I am sure it was, and I should not be pestering you about it. But I think Mrs. Carter is lovely, and I would hate for you to dismiss her out of an unfounded misunderstanding of her disposition."

Now Wyatt smiled. He knew the older woman was trying to be kind in a backward kind of way. The fact that it made him exceedingly uncomfortable was due to his own issues, and he ought not to take it out on her.

"I will think about what you've said, Mrs. Jenkins. I appreciate your kindness in wishing me well. But now I must be on my way, and you must continue on bed rest for at least one more day. I am happy with how the wound looks, but it has not healed sufficiently for you to be up and about."

Mrs. Jenkins made a face at him. "Maybe I don't wish you as much happiness as I said earlier."

The doctor laughed. "I understand. You take good care of yourself, Mrs. Jenkins, and I will see you tomorrow."

He gathered up his bag of supplies and made his way outside, preoccupied by his conversation with Mrs. Jenkins. It was extremely rare that he discussed his wife. No one here in Bucklin had known her, so it never came up in conversation. Most assumed he had never married, he was sure. And even back home, out East, no one who DID know would make conversation about her, thinking they were respecting his loss.

"But they don't even comprehend my loss, Boss." He knew it didn't speak well of his mindset for him to be talking to his horse, but the beast was an excellent listener, and Wyatt found himself in need of expressing his thoughts.

"The guilt I feel about her death is what's hard to manage. I should have been able to help her. I'm a doctor for goodness' sake. But not only could I not find her a cure, I couldn't even help her be happy. She was my best friend, and I failed her. Is it any wonder I don't think remarrying is the best idea?" The only response Boss provided was the rapid twitching of his ears, as though he really was listening.

"And I know you and Mrs. Jenkins think I'm attracted to Mrs. Carter, but I'm not." The horse's ears flicked back causing Wyatt to chuckle. "Alright, maybe I am, but it's just a normal physical reaction to how beautiful and healthy she is. I'm sure every man in town has noticed her. It doesn't change the fact that she's far too independent for my tastes." There was another flick of the horse's ears. Wyatt grinned. "I don't care how helpful she was yesterday with Mrs. Jenkins. The woman is trouble, and that's all I'm going to say on the subject." He laughed and shook his head at himself. Surely he was losing his mind.

Chapter Ten

"How are you feeling today, Mrs. Jenkins? I'm glad you have someone here to help you. Your granddaughter seems lovely."

"Good morning, Mrs. Carter. I'm right glad to lay eyes on you — let me tell you. Yes, Grace is a dear, but she doesn't have very much to say for herself. Thank you for stopping by."

"Are you up for company? Has the doctor given you the all clear to be moving about?"

"Bah, the doctor acts like I'm on death's door. He says I'm to stay in bed until he gives me leave to move about."

"Well, then shouldn't you be in bed?" Katie was startled by the older woman's seeming energy. She couldn't bear to have a repeat of the other day's experience.

"Don't look so worried, dear. I'm not overdoing it — I promise you. I just cannot see or hear much of anything up in my bed. Doctor Jeffries said it would be all right for me to be down here as long as I sit still."

"It doesn't look to me that you're sitting still."

Mrs. Jeffries let out a bark of laughter. "I promise not to faint on you. And I will keep myself in this chair. I probably won't be much use if you're wanting to do any measuring of me, but if you have some material samples, I would be giddy with delight."

Katie giggled at the older woman's words. "I did bring some swatches with me, as a matter of fact. Should I get you a cup of tea while we look at them?"

"Mrs. Carter, you are an angel."

Katie trilled with laughter again. "Surely by now you ought to be calling me Katie. I am certain we are to be good friends."

Mrs. Jenkins flushed with delight over Katie's words. "It would be an honor. And you must call me Althea. Or Thea, as my dearly departed used to say."

"Very well, Thea, I'm pleased to make your acquaintance." Katie shook her hand solemnly before grinning like a simpleton and then hurrying from the room. It was hard to believe that the crusty old lady was quickly becoming her closest friend.

With steaming cups of tea settled before them, the two women began sorting through the fabric samples Katie had brought with her.

"You have quite the selection, Katie, dear. I'm impressed."

"We have been fortunate thus far. The few women of Bucklin have been generous in the use of our services. So we have many scraps to make the swatches from. And the mercantile has a remarkably good stock for the size of this town. The shopkeeper has promised me that he'll be getting even more in, to keep us supplied. And if we don't yet have exactly what you want, we could probably get it ordered in, as well."

"Oh no, my dear girl, it looks to me like I'll be able to find exactly what I want from these materials. I have been more than happy with the first dress you made for me. But my daughter has been after me for so long about my need for new clothes. Now she says one new dress isn't enough." Mrs. Jenkins shook her head over the folly of the younger generation. "It's not as though I go around very much. No one is going to be looking at me."

"But you want to look good for your own enjoyment, don't you? I can assure you, while I wouldn't want to affront anyone's eyes with a decrepit appearance, I dress well for myself. I don't really care what anyone else thinks. I like looking good for me."

"And it doesn't hurt if it catches the eyes of a few gentlemen, does it?" Mrs. Jenkins teased her.

Katie blushed. "To be honest, I would rather gentlemen didn't look at me."

"Why ever not? You are young and beautiful. You should be trying to snag a good man."

"No, I shouldn't. If I thought it would keep them away, I would dress in a sack," Katie insisted.

"That hardly seems reasonable, Katie."

Katie shrugged. "You do know I've already been married, right?"

Mrs. Jenkins blinked at the question. "Well, we do call you Mrs. Carter on occasion, so I guess I must have known. Are you a runaway?"

Katie laughed, but it was a little hollow. "Not at all. I am a widow. My husband caught the flu and brought it home with him. He and our baby died within a couple days of each other."

"Oh, my dear, that is tragic. I am so sorry for your loss." There was a quiet moment while they both brushed a tear away. Mrs. Jenkins cleared her throat before asking, "How long has it been, my dear?"

"Two years, four months, and sixteen days since my sweet baby was taken from me. He was only nine months old, but he was such a charming little boy."

"I can only imagine how lovely a son of yours would be. He would have grown up to be a fine man, I'm sure."

Katie's smile was wan. "I struggled with wondering if he would, to be perfectly honest with you, Thea. While he was a sweet and happy baby, his father was less than kind, and it had troubled me terribly to wonder what he would grow up to be. Now I'll never know. I almost died from my grief. It's how I ended up with the orphans. I thought it would fill the hole in my heart where my baby used to be."

"Did it work?"

With another empty laugh, Katie shook her head. "Not really. But it filled my life with purpose, which was at least something. It saved my life. But it also broke a bit of what little heart I had left, which is part of why I needed the fresh start here in Bucklin. I couldn't take it anymore, seeing all the tragedy that the poor children faced, so I jumped at the chance to come out with the train of orphans and try a new life away from New York."

"But what about the hole in your heart? Surely finding a new love and having more babies is just what you need."

Shaking her head vigorously, Katie denied her friend's words. "Not at all. While no one could ever replace my sweet baby, now that I have my dear daughter, Annie, I am at peace. I have no need for a husband. In fact, I am far better off without one."

"I would beg to differ with you," Althea argued.

Grinning, Katie asked, "Why?"

"While men can be messy and stinky and annoying at times, there's nothing like having a partner as you walk through whatever life throws at you. Mr. Jenkins was an excellent father to my children and a steady companion for me. He worked hard to provide food and shelter for me and the children, but he always took the time to attend to any one of us. I think it's a good part of why our children grew up to be such wonderful adults. A good man is worth picking up after," she concluded with a girlish giggle.

Katie's smile was a little sad as she said, "Maybe so, but he's mighty hard to find."

The shrewd look Althea cast at her brought a lump to her throat. "Not so terribly hard, I'd say. I don't know many who aren't."

"Well then you've been far luckier in life than I have, Althea. I don't know very many men who are."

"I take it your marriage wasn't a happy one, then," Thea commented, her usually strident tones softened. "What about your parents?"

Katie shrugged again. "While not as bad as my husband, my father was cold and distant. He wasn't very pleased about having daughters, I think. There were four of us girls before my mother finally had two sons. From what I can tell, he had gotten pretty bitter by then, and my brothers didn't turn it around very much. They weren't very healthy. My father blamed my mother for that instead of the poor circumstances we were living in. Both of my brothers, my parents, and one of my sisters died in the past ten years. I'm glad I'm not living in the stews of the city anymore."

"You sure have faced more than your share of tragedy in your short life, Katie dear. But going it alone isn't the solution."

"There isn't a problem that needs a solution, here, though, Thea. I'm more than satisfied with the life I'm building here in Bucklin with Melanie and Annie."

"But what if Melanie finds a husband?"

"Well, then there will be more room in the house for me and Annie," she laughed.

"But what about when Annie grows up? Surely you don't want to grow old alone."

"Like you're doing?" Katie asked gently.

"I'm not alone," Althea declared with a chuckle. "I have a big, beautiful family. And while my poor Mr. Jenkins is no longer with me, I have so many wonderful memories to keep me company."

Katie knew her smile was wistful but couldn't help it. "That's lovely, Thea, but I think it's very rare."

"I don't," the older woman insisted again. "And I don't think you should be so cynical at your young age, despite the tragedy you've faced. You really ought to give love a chance. It's worth everything once you've found it."

Katie gazed out the window, debating whether or not to open herself up to her new friend. She never spoke of her past to anyone. Not even Melanie knew the extent of what she had suffered. She didn't have to tell Thea everything, but maybe if she told her some of her experiences it would get her to forget about trying to find a husband for her.

She took a deep breath and proceeded. "I had just turned seventeen the week before I got married. My husband was so very handsome. That's all I had the sense to think of when I was so young. And he was so attentive. Coming around to visit me every day, wanting to know who I had been with that day, who I had spoken with. He hated to hear if I had spoken with any other man. Even my brothers. I thought his jealousy meant he truly loved me. I found out later it just meant he was a jealous person."

Her next deep breath was a little shuddery, but Althea hadn't said anything, so she continued. "He was a few years older than me. I thought he was wonderful. So handsome and experienced. And I was so happy to get away from my dull existence at home. But he used all that supposed experience to squash my youthful exuberance. After the first couple of weeks, he began to tell me how stupid I was. That I wasn't doing anything right. The apartment wasn't how he wanted it kept. The meals weren't cooked to his preference. And when I didn't get pregnant immediately, well that had to be because something was wrong with me, too."

Katie again paused, staring out the window at the swaying trees. She absently thought about Annie, hoping she had on a warm enough sweater. Althea still hadn't commented on Katie's story, and Katie didn't look at her. Her voice was strong despite her desire to crawl into a hole and not come out for at least a week after reliving these memories. Now that she had started, it seemed she couldn't stem the flow of words.

"He didn't hit me right at first. He stole all my joy and enthusiasm first. I almost never saw anyone in my family after the first few months. I *never* saw any of my old friends after the first couple of weeks. It wasn't worth the fighting. But just when I thought things had settled down and I was keeping him satisfied, he started drinking. And that's when he started hitting me. It was always my fault, of course. Or so he told me. I believed him at the time. I thought I was going to die several times. I wished I would die many times.

"When we realized that I was pregnant, he didn't hit me as often, nor as severely, for which I was grateful. Until right near the end of my pregnancy. Because I was so ungainly, I was clumsy and awkward. He didn't like that at all. Then he didn't want me to see a doctor because he didn't want anyone to see me like that. But I convinced him we could say I fell down the stairs and that we had to get help because the baby was coming. When my water broke, he finally believed me and went for help. I was profoundly relieved when the baby was born quickly and perfect. He gave me a reason to live. Until my husband brought the flu home and took the baby from me. I wasn't in the least sorry when he died."

Her eyes flew up. "My husband, I mean. I wanted to die myself when the baby died. I can still hear the rattle of his breaths as he gasped for air. There was nothing I could do. The doctor wouldn't even come into our neighborhood since the sickness was such a pandemic. No one could help me because anyone who was still standing had too many patients of their own to care for. I don't know which cruel providence spared me from death, but I didn't even get a sniffle. I was weak as a kitten by the time it was all over, but that was from crying myself dry over the baby and not sleeping at all from caring for my husband and child, as well as my sister. My sister made it. The others didn't. She was left a little damaged after the illness, but she's still alive to this day."

Katie finally looked up to meet Althea's gaze. Her own eyes were dry, but Thea's were streaming with tears. "I didn't have any tears left after my baby died. Not even when my mother passed. Once it became obvious that I wasn't going to be getting sick, and after most of my family had been buried, I started volunteering at the orphanage. I thought being with the children would help me feel close to my own sweet Henry. It sort of did. It helped me heal. Children are a gift to the world, even when their circumstances are tragic, like the orphans. But as I regained my sense of self, my tolerance for the suffering I was witnessing all around me began to decrease. By the time I had lost most of my numbness, I could no longer remain in New York. When I was asked to accompany the children to Missouri, I jumped at the chance to start fresh."

Katie took another deep breath, this time feeling restored, as though telling her story had lanced the wound. "And now that I have been blessed with another child, I feel whole again. I would never want to take the risk of marriage again. Too much is at stake."

∞

Wyatt felt his jaw clench over what he had heard. He knew he shouldn't be eavesdropping. He hadn't even meant to. But when he had been about to knock, he had heard Katie's clear voice coming through the open window. And he had hesitated. Just long enough to hear what they were talking about. And when he realized what it was, he couldn't interrupt. There's no way Katie would talk about any of this in front of him. From what he knew of her, he was amazed she was talking about it with Mrs. Jenkins. But hearing what she had been through made everything in him clench, not just his jaw. His stomach burned. His hands were inadvertently forming into fists. A part of him wanted to give her husband a taste of what he had been doling out. Not that Katie would welcome more violence. She probably wouldn't welcome him having this knowledge either. He really ought to alert the women to his presence. But he just wanted to hear a little bit more. It explained so much about the woman's prickly response to him. Why would she welcome any contact with a man after what she'd experienced?

"But don't you think Annie would benefit from having a man helping to raise her? Don't shake your head at me, young lady." Wyatt almost gave away his presence with a snort of laughter over Mrs.

Jenkins' tone. "You might not think she needs a father, after the rough ride you've had, but surely you could use help. I've always thought God knew what he was doing when he arranged for a father and mother. No matter how capable you are, you are only one person. Raising a family is hard work."

"I'm sure it would be ideal for her to have a father, but I will do everything in my power to be enough for her. At least there's only one child, so I won't be outnumbered. And her teacher is a man, so she won't lack for a different perspective."

Katie paused, and Wyatt wished he could see her face to try to figure out what she was really thinking.

"I understand what you're trying to say, Thea, and I appreciate you sharing your thoughts with me, but I think we might just have to agree to disagree on this one. I cannot take the chance now, even more so than before. I would never forgive myself if I brought someone into Annie's life only to have him hurt her."

Mrs. Jenkins made a sound of protest, and Wyatt realized he had learned enough from the conversation he had overheard. He really needed to make his presence known before they caught him spying. With some exaggerated clomping of his feet, he made his way to the door and knocked.

When Mrs. Jenkins' granddaughter opened the door, he wasn't even surprised to see Katie hastily grabbing her bag and kissing Mrs. Jenkins' cheek goodbye.

"I'll stop in again in a couple days. Hopefully by then your tyrant of a doctor will have given you the all clear for moving around." Katie tried to make a light joke, but Wyatt could see that her smile didn't quite reach her eyes. His heart ached for the pain he could see reflected in their depths.

"Good day, Mrs. Carter." He greeted her with a slight bow, chuckling when pink stained her cheeks.

"Doctor Jeffries." She nodded at him before scurrying away.

He stood, staring at the door after it closed behind her retreating form. He turned back to face Mrs. Jenkins.

"Was it something I said?"

She grinned at him. "You know perfectly well that it's something she said."

Wyatt felt all the blood drain from his face before it quickly returned with full heat. "You knew I was there?" he demanded.

"Of course," she retorted. "I might be getting old, but nothing gets past me."

"Did she know?"

If he hadn't been so embarrassed, he would have laughed over the withering look she cast him. "Do you really think she would have said any of that if she knew?"

The answer was so obvious that Wyatt didn't even reply.

Mrs. Jenkins continued studying him like a specimen in a science lab. "Does it make you like her any more now that you know why she's so independent?"

Wyatt smiled. "It's not a matter of not liking her, Mrs. Jenkins. I think Mrs. Carter is a lovely woman, despite her modern ideals. I understand her a little better now that I know about her past. But that doesn't mean I could live with those ideals. Yes, the strength of character she has displayed in order to survive and even thrive after what she has been through might be attractive. But a man wants to feel needed by a woman he's going to take for his wife. And he doesn't want to have to fear having his ears blistered whenever he does something not quite to her liking."

"Has Katie ever blistered your ears?"

Wyatt gave a half shrug.

"You're thinking about your wife again and putting that on her, aren't you?" Mrs. Jenkins asked shrewdly.

Wyatt sidestepped the question with one of his own. "Have you met the woman Mrs. Carter is living with? I believe she arrived on the same train."

"Now don't be getting any ideas about her, Doctor Jeffries. I know you think you want a meek and mild wife sitting home keeping your supper warm for you, but you need a woman who isn't afraid to speak her mind or leave the house once in a while. No, I haven't met Miss Melanie yet. While she has a way with her needle, I don't think it's normal that she has barely set foot outside their door." Mrs. Jenkins shook her head and interrupted whatever Wyatt was about to say. "No, you might not agree with how Katie has dealt with her past experiences, but at least she's dealing with them. And as sociable as you are, you need someone who can accompany you, not someone who is going to shrink into your shadow."

Wyatt frowned over Mrs. Jenkins' words, wondering if there was wisdom in them. She surely had seen more of life than he had, despite living in this small town. He hesitated to accept them, though. He couldn't picture a peaceful future with the small but mighty Mrs. Carter.

"Well, never mind about my quest for a wife, Mrs. Jenkins, tell me how you're feeling today."

"I am feeling like a new woman with the entertainment I've been provided between you and the dear, sweet Mrs. Carter." She cackled over her words before growing serious. "But I'm pretty sure my nasty boils are healing up now. Surely you'll let me get up soon."

"Well, let me take a look, and I'll let you know."

Chapter Eleven

"Hello? Mrs. Mitchell?" Katie called out from the doorway. She checked her watch. Eleven o'clock. She was right on time. "It's Katie, Mrs. Mitchell. We had an appointment for me to take your measurements?"

"Help me! Please!" Katie heard a young voice coming from the back of the house. She dropped her bag of supplies and ran in that direction, skidding to a stop when she came across the boy standing over Mr. and Mrs. Mitchell's prone bodies. He looked terrified. "It's the flu, isn't it?" he demanded.

Katie's stomach turned over, and she wanted to run back in the direction she had come from. If she never heard those words again for the rest of her life, it would be too soon. She took a deep breath and did what needed to be done.

"Hello. My name's Mrs. Carter, what's yours?"

"I'm Matt. Can you help them? Please don't let them die."

"I'll do my best, Matt. How old are you?"

"I'm ten."

"That's great. That means you're a big boy, right?"

He finally tore his eyes away from staring at Mr. and Mrs. Mitchell and looked at Katie. He stood a little straighter as he nodded agreement.

"Excellent. Now, I need you to go find the doctor. Don't get too close to anyone while you're going through town, just in case it *is* the flu. You're one of the boys we brought on the train, aren't you?"

Matt nodded before his eyes skittered back to looking at Mr. and Mrs. Mitchell. "I don't want to lose them. I just got here."

Katie's heart squeezed with the thought of what this boy had already endured in his young life. She needed him to be brave just a little bit more. She offered him an encouraging smile.

"I know, Matt, we're going to do our very best. Somehow, you and I got lucky and we don't get this particular sickness. So we'll be able to help them if that is what they have. Now, go find the doctor so he can help us."

She couldn't believe she was voluntarily sending for the doctor, but she knew she couldn't face this on her own. And Katie was fairly certain the doctor would want to be involved in preventing the spread of the dreadful disease in this town. Her stomach turned over as she wondered if the train passengers had brought this terrible thing with them. She shook herself out of her momentary inertia. While she wanted to run away, she had a neighborly obligation to do the best she could for the Mitchells. She didn't know if she would be able to deal with any more death from this dreadful disease on an emotional level, but there wasn't much she could do about that now. She was involved. It just had to be dealt with. At least she didn't have to fear that she would bring it home to Annie. It would seem the child was also immune, since she had survived what had wiped out her family.

Katie set herself in motion, hoping Matt was able to return quickly with the doctor or some other responsible adult in tow. Her fears were besetting her. She had to shake it off and do what she could for the Mitchells.

She was in the midst of spooning lukewarm broth into Mrs. Mitchell's mouth when she finally heard the arrival of Doctor Jeffries and Matt. Katie felt a sigh of relief leave her before her anxieties returned once more. On top of her concerns for the Mitchells, she now had to cope with the uncomfortable presence of the doctor. Even though she had requested his help, she dreaded being around him.

"Katie?" the doctor questioned informally before quickly asking, "Are you all right, Mrs. Carter?"

With a tight smile, she nodded at him. There was a beat of silence before she responded. "Thanks for coming. I'm sorry for needing to involve you in this, but I can't face it completely on my own. I would actually rather not deal with this at all, but I could not walk away when

I realized Matt was here on his own. I'm afraid it is as he suspected, the flu. They both have the rash, and they're burning up with fever."

While the doctor absorbed this information, Katie turned to the boy, who had followed the doctor into the room. "Were you able to get the doctor without getting too close to anyone else?"

The boy nodded vigorously. "Very good, Matt. Thank you. If you would, I have another task for you to perform. Could you take a note for me to my house?"

Poor Matt looked thrilled at the thought of not needing to stay in the room with his ill adoptive parents. He quickly ran to find a piece of paper and a pencil for Katie to write her note.

"Tell me what you have done so far," the doctor demanded, getting down to business.

"I set a pot on the stove. While that was heating up I bathed their faces and chests and then changed their bedding." Katie forced herself to be as stoic as possible, but she could still feel heat climbing in her cheeks with embarrassment over performing the very personal task for two people she barely knew. "I have since been trying to get as much of the broth into them as I could. From my experience, that's all that can be done for the fever. I really hope you have some other ideas."

"You have done well. Unfortunately, if this is the flu, there isn't much else that can be done. We can just keep doing what you've started. Keeping fluids in them will be the most gruelling task," he pointed out as Mrs. Mitchell threw up all that Katie had managed to get into her so far. It hadn't been much, and Katie had had the foresight to put a towel around the woman's neck, so all her efforts of cleaning the woman hadn't come undone.

Mrs. Mitchell moaned softly, but Katie just murmured gently to her. The older woman quieted and drifted deeper into sleep.

"Sleep and fluids will be what will save them."

Katie quickly wrote a note to Melanie, letting her know where she was and asking that she look after Annie for the foreseeable future. *I have no idea how long I will have to remain here*, she wrote. *I would rather not be here, but someone has to do it. Don't come by, and don't let Annie visit. She survived it once — I don't want to take any chances, nor do I want her to be frightened. Try to satisfy her by telling her I'm helping out some friends. I dearly hope I won't be too long.*

"How well do you know the Mitchells, doctor?" Katie asked after she had sent Matt off with her note.

"Fairly well," he answered. "It's a small town. Most everyone knows everything about everyone. Why do you ask?"

"Do they have any family we should send for to care for them?"

"Would you want to risk others?" He was incredulous.

"No, of course not, but I cannot remain here for too long."

"Why not?"

Katie started to feel frustrated with him. "For one thing, I don't think being in your company is going to be pure pleasure, and for another, I have a child to take care of. A fact that you have been repeatedly reminding me of, if you'll recall. And I did my duty with my own family with this dreadful disease. I'm not sure if my mind and heart can bear up under doing it again."

The doctor was grinning over her words when she first started talking, as though her show of spirit amused him, but he sobered at her reminder of what she had lost to the dreadful disease.

"Of course, I understand. We'll have a good idea in the next few hours what the future will hold for these two, so we'll have more answers as to whether or not we'll need help. As it stands, I would rather not involve anyone else. I will be able to remain even if you cannot do so."

Katie didn't appreciate his condescending tone even as he professed to understand her reasons for not wanting to be there. But there was little she could do. Even though she wanted to be anywhere but there, she knew in her heart, she could never abandon the Mitchells. She would much rather pass their care off to a family member, but she understood the doctor not wanting to risk anyone else's health. She just hoped her surprising immunity to the dreadful disease held. Katie offered him a tight smile and without a word left the room to go boil more water.

ঙ০জ্ঞ

Wyatt watched through the window as Katie struggled to get the heavy bedding over the line to dry. He shouldn't be referring to her so familiarly, even in his head, since she had not given him leave to do so, but he couldn't help himself. It had now been twenty-four hours that they had been here together, watching over poor Mr. and Mrs. Mitchell. And poor Matt. The boy was trying to hide his fears, but it was obvious that he was terrified. Wyatt couldn't blame him. He now realized that Matt's entire family had been wiped out as the plague of influenza had swept through New York. That was how he wound up an orphan on the train out to Missouri. The same was true of Mrs. Carter. It was interesting to watch the two bond over their shared losses.

His attention had been wandering, but his focus was brought back to Katie as she snapped another sheet in the breeze before tossing it over the line. Wyatt wouldn't have thought it possible, but the small woman was even more beautiful today, with tendrils of hair flying wildly about her head after having escaped her tight hair style.

The doctor was amazed that she had remained. He knew she didn't want to be there. But she hadn't wavered in her care of the Mitchells. Wyatt knew it was his job, as the doctor, to care for people. Katie was only doing it out of neighborly duty. She barely even knew the Mitchells. He was deeply impressed with her diligence.

Despite his previous declaration that women should stay home and tend the family fires, there was no arguing with the fact that he would have been seriously challenged to handle this medical case on his own. Two seriously ill patients and a terrified boy would have been beyond his abilities, he was man enough to admit. But he suspected that even if he wasn't there, the brave little widow would have managed on her own. He didn't want to respect her, and he most certainly didn't want to have feelings for her, but he could feel his heart rate picking up as he stood there, watching her doing something so pragmatic as hanging the laundry out to dry. For the briefest moment, he allowed himself to picture her doing such a task at his own house. He quickly shut the idea down. He doubted she would consider it and, he reminded himself, he didn't want such an independent soul as his mate.

But he had a welcoming smile on his lips when she returned to the house. It turned to amusement as she cast him a suspicious glare.

"Why are you looking at me like that?" she demanded, keeping her voice low so as not to disturb the others in the house, but conveying her discomfort quite clearly as she set aside the basket she had been carrying. "I know I'm not the prettiest picture, but you are quite aware of what I have been experiencing in the last day besides not sleeping, so you needn't look at me so."

He protested. "I swear to you, I was not looking at you in judgement of any sort. Quite the contrary, in fact. I was just thinking that I would not have been able to handle this situation without you."

The look of surprise that swept across her features made him want to laugh out loud, but he managed to restrain the impulse, realizing that it would cause her to leave the house in anger.

"Well, thank you," she answered grudgingly. "I wouldn't have been able to do it alone, either," she admitted. There was a pause while she couldn't meet his gaze before she continued. "To be honest, I think if I had been left alone here, while I wouldn't want to abandon them to their fate, I'm not sure if I would have been able to handle it. My fears would have overwhelmed me. I think of how it was when I was on my own with Mrs. Jenkins after she fainted. And that was just a few days ago. I don't think I could have borne it again so soon. Even having Matt here wouldn't have been enough to keep me grounded, since the poor boy is struggling so hard to control his own fears. Having a real doctor present is keeping him comforted. If he had only me, I don't think the two of us would fare well."

Wyatt chuckled, which brought a glare from her, and hot color flooded her cheeks. It only subsided as he soothed, "I, on the other hand, think you would have fared as well as was needed. You seem to be one of those remarkable people who manage to do whatever needs to be done. You managed just fine with Mrs. Jenkins, and you're doing wonderfully here."

He admired her beauty as her cheeks remained a light pink but this time out of embarrassment as she turned bashful. "Thank you, Doctor Jeffries, that's kind of you to say. But while I have an aversion to doctors out of principle, I have to say I'm in the same camp as Matt. Having someone present who has actually been formally educated in the art of medicine is a comfort in this situation. In New York, when the plague was running rampant, there were far too many patients and not nearly enough doctors. And when your pockets were to let, there was no hope for you. You had to muddle through as best you could with only prayer and hot water on your side. And clean water was even hard to come by. That is one beautiful luxury out here in Missouri. It doesn't seem that anyone is concerned about water."

She stopped talking for a moment, but Wyatt didn't comment. Despite having worked side by side now on two occasions, this was the most the independent woman had shared in one sitting. He hoped she would continue. He was finding it singularly fascinating. And he was bored silly from watching their two patients sleep. His patience was rewarded when she offered him a small, sheepish smile.

"Do you know, I awaken each morning in such a thankful frame of mind as I drink a large cup of the sweet water that comes from the well behind our little house. Melanie does the same thing. Neither of us can quite believe how much water is around. And it's so clean. And sweet. Of course, I still love my tea, but it feels almost decadent to be able to drink fresh, cool water and not fear that it might make you sick if you don't boil it first. Thankfully, Annie is too young to have been filled with the fears we had. I think her parents must have done a wonderful job of keeping most things from her. The poor little dear has enough fears as it is."

"Don't I know it," Wyatt interjected with a wry grin.

The color rose in her cheeks once again making his heart feel like it was turning over within his chest. "I'm sorry she hasn't been very friendly toward you. She sees doctors only as a source of bad news or who attend you when you're sick or injured."

"Most would be happy to have someone attend you when you've been injured," he pointed out.

"But the bad news overpowers any help you might have to offer, I'm afraid. I personally haven't had many dealings with doctors, previously. But my impression has been that doctors consider themselves to be gods sent to help those with the deepest pockets."

"That's terrible. And inaccurate of most doctors," Wyatt insisted, growing disappointed with the direction of the conversation.

She shrugged. "By saying it's inaccurate of most, you are admitting that it's not inaccurate of all doctors."

He grudgingly nodded. "Maybe not."

She smiled, apparently pleased with his honesty. "Perhaps, if we manage to help the Mitchells pull through, I'll invite you for dinner and you can tell Annie all about our success here. It might help her if she can see you as a bearer of glad tidings."

"Since I've had the pleasure of a sample of your good cooking here for the Mitchells, I will gladly accept," he replied with a chuckle.

He looked at her carefully and didn't much like what he saw at that moment. She was, of course, still beautiful, but he could see that the only color on her face was from her bashfulness over his compliment. Her eyes looked strained, and her mouth turned down at the edges when she wasn't smiling.

"Mrs. Carter, you really must take a break and get some sleep. I am feeling more confident that Mr. and Mrs. Mitchell are going to pull through this illness. It won't do for you to collapse as they are improving. You must take some rest."

For a brief moment, she looked as though she were going to be mulish and refuse, but then she offered him a sheepish smile. "Are you certain you'll be able to remain awake if I lie down for a bit?"

"I'll keep Matt with me, and we'll watch over them while you sleep. Then you can take a turn after you've rested a bit."

Her face filled with relief as she accepted his offer. "You're probably right. I won't be any good for Annie when this is over either, if I go and get sick myself. Thank you, doctor."

Wyatt watched as she slipped from the room. She was so slender she almost floated, he thought whimsically. He shook his head and derided himself. *You're a fool*, he thought, *you don't want her, but you can't stop thinking about her. Make up your mind, man.* Then he had to push all thoughts of her from his mind as he became fully occupied with keeping Matt reassured while the two of them cared for his adoptive parents.

A couple hours later, Katie slipped quietly into the room and startled them when she spoke up from the doorway.

"How are you two holding up? I never meant to sleep for so long. You must be nearly falling over with exhaustion."

"I'm not tired at all, Mrs. Carter. I slept all night, remember?"

The smile Katie offered to Matt nearly took Wyatt's breath away, but he managed to answer her calmly. "I haven't fallen over quite yet, but if my checker skills are anything to go by, my mind is not functioning at its best."

"Have you eaten? Would you like me to make you something before you go to sleep, or would you rather wait until you get back up?"

"Thank you for your kindness, Mrs. Carter. Matt and I have managed to look after ourselves fairly well. I think sleep is my priority at the moment."

She nodded her acceptance but had one more question. "Have you fed them?" she nodded quietly toward their patients.

"We gave them some tea about an hour ago. If you could get them to take some broth, that would be great." He was already leaving the room when he answered her. He was barely conscious as he climbed the stairs and collapsed on Matt's bed in the attic of the small house.

Chapter Twelve

After the doctor left, Katie struggled against feeling disappointed. She didn't want to enjoy his company and *definitely* didn't want to find him attractive. But she did have eyes in her head, she thought with a small smile. It couldn't be avoided that the man was good looking. And watching him care for his patients held a certain appeal. His patience with Matt had seemed endless. She admired his calm in the face of the various emergencies she had witnessed with him.

But the fact was that since she had met him, she had encountered three medical emergencies. Katie tried to be reasonable and pointed out to herself that with or without the doctor Mrs. Jenkins would have fainted, Annie would have knocked herself out, and the Mitchells would have gotten sick. Having the doctor there had helped, she had to admit. *Well, maybe not with Annie*, she protested silently. He did very little to help there. In fact, his lectures had only served to anger her and did nothing to aid the patient. But with Althea and here with the Mitchells he was invaluable.

While she didn't really want to be the one playing nurse, she was in agreement with the doctor that since she had already been exposed, it wouldn't serve to risk anyone else. She was just grateful that she was still feeling fit. Tired, yes, but still healthy. But she had been deeply relieved when Melanie had stopped at the gate that morning. Katie thought back to their brief conversation, smiling that it had been conducted with an entire yard between them.

'I've brought you a beef pie. You and the doctor need to keep your strength up. I'll just leave it here.'

"Thank you, Melanie. How are you and Annie faring? Did she have many questions?"

"It's Annie, she had plenty of questions, but don't fret, she's untroubled so far. If you're gone too long, though, I'm not sure how long that will last."

Katie chewed her lip in thought. *"If you must, you can bring her by like this so she can see that I'm fine."*

"I've done one better than that," Melanie had declared with a conspiratorial grin. *"I girded my courage and approached the father of one of her classmates to arrange a sleepover. Since there's no school tomorrow, she will be going home with Mary after classes. I won't have to face her questions until Sunday."*

"Melanie, thank you so much. I know that must have been a challenge for you, but it was brilliantly done of you."

Melanie shrugged. *"Apparently, they just had a litter of puppies, so I thought they'd be the best draw. But I cannot promise she won't be asking for a pet after this."*

The two friends shared a giggle before Melanie sobered. *"Are you doing all right? You look a little wrung out."*

"I didn't sleep through the night. So I'm plenty tired, but I think I'm faring fine. I can't say that I'm loving the experience, but I think poor little Matt would be beside himself if not for my familiar face."

"You're an angel of mercy, Katie."

"Don't go getting carried away, my friend." Katie was embarrassed by her words and quickly waved them away, changing the subject. *"I'll see you soon. Thank you so much for the food. We've been so occupied with the sick that I haven't been able to concentrate on keeping us fed. This will help so much."*

Now it was Mel's turn to look uncomfortable. *"It was the least I could do. You're the one doing all the hard work and taking the risk."*

They shared a laugh over their mutual discomfort. Melanie, still grinning, waved and walked away.

The meat pie had been delicious. And Melanie's generous portions meant that there was plenty left over for another meal.

Katie was relieved that Melanie had thought to speak with Mary's father. She hadn't wanted to ask it of her, knowing how she was still struggling with speaking to people, especially men. But with the litter of puppies, Mary was the friend most likely to keep Annie sufficiently occupied that she wouldn't be overly worried about her new mother's absence.

Living in a small town was proving to be a blessing for them. Everyone was so kind and willing to help out. The voice calling from the gate was a testament to that.

"Hello there," Katie heard a questioning note from the feminine voice.

"Grace? What are you doing here?" Katie asked when she opened the screen door.

"Grandmother heard that you've been caring for the Mitchells and asked me to bring over some soup for you."

"That is mighty kind of the both of you. Thank you. And please tell your grandmother thank you from us, as well. Soup will come in handy as the Mitchells start to recover."

"So they're on the mend, then, are they? The townspeople are wondering," the girl added.

"We're fairly confident that the worst has passed," Katie assured her. "But it's best if everyone stays away for a while longer."

The girl nodded vigorously, relief clearly written across her face. Katie's heart went out to her. "It was brave of you to do your grandmother's bidding," she said, keeping her tone low enough not to carry far, but loud enough for the girl to hear. Grace nodded shyly before scurrying away.

The large pot of soup was going to be such an aid to them. They were nearly out of the broth she had made the day before. After the next meal they gave to the Mitchells, they would be out. She had been thinking of rationing it until she was able to make more, but now she wouldn't have to. And it would do them good to have a little bit more substance with soup instead of just broth.

Katie wondered if they would even be feeding the Mitchells anymore. They seemed to be regaining consciousness and were even moving a little bit. Surely they would be waking up soon. She certainly hoped the doctor was awake as well when they did.

Matt interrupted her musings.

"Can I do anything, Mrs. Carter?"

Katie gave him a warm smile. "What would you be doing if your parents hadn't fallen sick?"

He shrugged. "I've already done most of the chores. I guess I would normally have homework to do. Or I would go play with some of the boys from school."

"I'm sorry that you have to stay away from your friends. This must be a boring ordeal for you."

The boy shrugged again. "I'm worried more than I'm bored."

"I know, Matt," she answered softly. "But why don't you go outside and play? Even by yourself, you should be able to find something to do. The fresh air and sunshine will do you good. And it'll make it easier for you to sleep tonight if you've had a bit of activity through the day."

"I don't think I'll have any trouble sleeping tonight," he replied with a grin. "I'm not used to doing all the chores by myself."

Now Katie was chagrinned. "Was it too much for you? I'm so sorry, Matt! I have been so preoccupied with caring for your parents that I haven't thought that much about the chores outside of the house. Should we get someone to come in and do some of them for us?"

Matt was quick to protest. "No, no, not at all, Mrs. Carter. I don't mind doing it one bit. It's harder work than I ever did back in New York, but I actually find it quite fun. And since I can't go to school, it gave me something to do."

"Of course. I sure hope this passes soon. I'm not making any sense at all, am I?" Katie waved a hand in front of her face, trying to distract herself from the tears wanting to form in her eyes.

Matt grinned at her. "I think I will go out and see if I can find any frogs."

Katie laughed. She was so glad she had adopted a girl, she thought with a slight shudder as the boy hurried to put his shoes on and ran from the room.

She was puttering around, tidying the house, when the doctor re-entered the room. She was preoccupied with scrubbing the stove and didn't hear him until he spoke.

"How have—" he began before she whirled around and stifled her squeal of fright.

With a hand upon her chest she panted. "Doctor Jeffries! You nearly scared the wits out of me."

He chuckled but quickly apologized. "I'm so sorry! I did not mean to startle you. I didn't realize cleaning the stove required quite that much concentration."

Katie had to laugh at his attempt at a joke. "It shouldn't require that much thought, you're right. But I'm exhausted, and everything is a challenge at this point."

He smiled in agreement, and her breath caught once more. The man was remarkably handsome in a studious kind of way. Being as tired as she was, her resistance was weak, and she found her heart rate was picking up from his proximity. She tried to hide her discomfort with activity, setting back to work scrubbing the stove.

"You don't really need to be doing so much work here, Mrs. Carter," the doctor admonished. "You are going to wear yourself out even more than necessary."

"If they pull through, Mr. and Mrs. Mitchell are going to be weak for some time. Mrs. Mitchell won't be able to do as much as she would no doubt usually do. I cannot think she would mind if I set the house to rights before I leave."

When she caught his gaze on her, she raised her eyebrows. "What?" she asked. "Don't you agree?"

"I do, and I am certain she will appreciate your thoughtfulness. I just didn't expect it from you."

Katie flushed. "Why not? Because I'm a single woman trying to make a home without a husband?" she demanded. "You're rather repetitious, doctor." She probably shouldn't have said that, but she couldn't bring herself to retract her words.

With a roll of his eyes, the doctor turned on his heel and left the room to check on his patients. Katie stared after his retreating back and bit her lip in indecision. She ought not to have been so defensive. Maybe that wasn't what he had meant at all. She wanted to follow him and apologize, but this was not the time or place for her personal feelings. They weren't there on a social visit. With a shake of her head, she returned to her task.

The rest of the day flew past as they continued to care for the Mitchells. They had both indeed regained consciousness and were awake and eating the soup Mrs. Jenkins had sent over.

"I cannot believe you have been here for two days caring for us," Mrs. Mitchell croaked past her raw throat.

"Don't try to talk too much — spare your energy," Katie protested, not wishing to be embarrassed by her thanks.

The woman looked as though she were going to protest, but then must have realized the wisdom in Katie's words as she slumped back onto her pillow with a weak smile and a nod.

By the time the ill couple had finished the soup and were sleeping again, Doctor Jeffries had decided they were well and truly on the mend. "You ought to go home and have a proper sleep, Mrs. Carter. You have gone above and beyond your neighborly duty and should feel free to leave them in my care now."

When Katie went to protest, the doctor overrode her. "I am sure the neighbors will bring more food. You bathed Mrs. Mitchell after her fever broke, changed the bedding, and have washed all the sheets. There is really nothing more for you to do here. And I want you to get a proper rest before you end up one of my patients."

Katie gave him a wry smile in reaction to his last words. "Are you very sure you will be able to manage without me?" She flushed with embarrassment and began to stammer. "That's not to say that I was so very useful, but an extra pair of hands and being a woman…" She trailed off as he began to chuckle at her expense. She wanted to resent his amusement but couldn't prevent her rueful smile.

"You were far more help than I could have hoped for, and I would have been in trouble if not for you. But yes, I am quite certain that the worst has passed and I can manage from here. If that changes, I promise to send Matt for you."

This finally mollified her, and she agreed to depart. With a start, though, she realized that it had already fallen dark. The doctor caught her apprehensive glance out the window as she gathered her few things and said farewell to Matt.

"Matt, will you be comfortable sitting with your parents while I escort Mrs. Carter home?" Doctor Jeffries asked the boy.

Before Matt could answer, Katie protested. "I am perfectly capable of walking home on my own."

"I am certain you are capable, my good woman — that is not a question. I would just be left to wonder if you had found your way successfully and would not be able to have a peaceful night for worrying. If you allow me to escort you home, with a lantern to light the way, we can all rest easy tonight."

When he put it like that, Katie feared it would be churlish to refuse. She offered him a helpless shrug and inclined her head in acceptance.

Matt had been nodding vigorously along with the doctor. "It's much better this way, Mrs. Carter. You never know what might be out there in the dark. I wouldn't want to be wandering about by myself. But I'll be fine here in the house until you get back Dr. Jeffries."

Katie grinned at the boy, picked up her small bag, and preceded the doctor from the house.

They walked along in companionable silence for a few minutes before the doctor remarked, "You must be anxious to get home to your daughter and your usual life."

"Oh, I have missed Annie almost unbearably, it's true. But there is something so satisfying about helping someone who is in such desperate need of aid. I think I envy you your profession, doctor. You get to have this experience every day."

ⅎℛ

Wyatt chuckled. "Luckily for the folks of Bucklin, there aren't people in dire need every single day. But you are right, it is an immensely satisfying way of life."

He couldn't decide if it was a reflection from the lantern or her own inner joy, but the lovely little woman at his side seemed to glow as they walked along.

"I'm sorry that I was resistant to the thought of staying when you first asked it of me. I am delighted that I was able to help poor Mr. and Mrs. Mitchell. They likely would have died if not for the train load of orphans, wouldn't you think?"

Wyatt lifted a questioning eyebrow and was rewarded by her sweet laughter drifting out. She quickly defended her position. "Think about it, doctor. If not for the train, I wouldn't have been knocking at their door. And they wouldn't have had Matt. Even if I hadn't come along when I did, I'm sure Matt would have realized he needed to go for help eventually. But if not for the train, he wouldn't have been there. No one might have noticed they were ill until it was too late."

"I guess you have a solid point there, Mrs. Carter. Besides the Mitchells, I'm sure there are many in this town who would consider the arrival of the train of orphans to be a godsend. You are certainly a positive addition to the company of our town."

Despite the dim light, Wyatt could see that her color was heightened. It was most becoming. He almost held his breath as he took in her beauty. He tried to be nonchalant. She bashfully kept her silence.

"What do you suppose you will do first when you get home?" he asked to change the subject.

"I've thought of burning my clothes, but I used to be fond of this gown, so I will try not to do anything so drastic."

Wyatt couldn't help but chuckle. "Why would you do something like that?"

"I have never gone so long without changing my clothes," she explained. "Almost three days, including sleeping in them," she said with a shudder. "I may not burn them, but the first thing I intend to do is have a thorough bath." She must have questioned the correctness of discussing this with him as she hurried to add, "And then I feel like I could sleep for a week. But probably being in my own room without keeping an ear open for anyone's moans, I'll be able to sleep like a rock and waken fresh as a daisy by morning."

"I certainly hope so." Wyatt almost moaned himself over the fervour in his tone. He didn't want her reading anything into his enthusiasm. He quickly tried to explain himself. "You were such a help — you deserve your rest."

"Thank you, doctor. I will take my sleep seriously, as doctor's orders."

He was surprised and heartened by her teasing tone. She always seemed so serious. He was glad to see her being playful. But it made his pulse quicken, which was not at all acceptable. Wyatt questioned the sanity of offering to escort her home, not that sending her off on her own would have been acceptable. He sighed heavily.

"That sigh sounded rather deeply genuine, doctor. Are you feeling all right?"

Her solicitous tone only served to make his pulse quicken further and his palms began to sweat. Maybe he was catching the fever the Mitchells had, he thought in desperation.

"I find I'm more tired than I had realized," he excused.

She made a sound of protest. "You ought not to be out here with me. I really could have managed on my own."

The doctor now offered an exaggeratedly heavy sigh. "I am well aware of just how capable you are, Mrs. Carter, but I can assure you, no gentleman of honor would allow you to traipse about the village on your own in the dark. While most members of our town are fine upstanding citizens, you can never be sure who might be passing through, besides the wild creatures you could encounter. Now quit your protests, and allow me to do my duty."

He could hear the disgruntled growl in his voice but wasn't prepared for the loud laugh that emitted from his companion. "Very well, doctor, I will cease resisting your assistance and will admit to you that I am relieved not to be out here in the dark alone. I am still not accustomed to the sounds of nature at night, and I would probably be beside myself with terror by now if not for you and your lantern."

There was a quiet pause while Wyatt quelled his surprise at her words and waited to see what else she would say. His patience was rewarded. "But I still feel badly that you are out here with me when you could be tucked up getting some rest."

"Don't pay it any mind, Mrs. Carter. A doctor's duty is often discharged in the wee hours of the night. It seems most illnesses wait for the night time to pounce. And babies love to arrive in the middle of the night as well."

Another gurgle of laughter followed his words, and Wyatt had to grin.

"So when do you ever sleep?" she questioned.

"It's a small town, Mrs. Carter, it certainly doesn't happen every night. But I've learned to take my sleep when I can get it. I have slept in the sunshine in an open field more times than I can count. In fact, the time I was late arriving when you were with Mrs. Jenkins was after the arrival of the Channing twins. It was a difficult labor, and I hadn't slept a wink, so on my way to Mrs. Jenkins' I came across an inviting patch of grass and meant to only take a couple of minutes, but it ended up being a couple of hours."

"Oh dear. That explains why your cheeks were so pink when you arrived. I hadn't really noticed at the time, since I was beside myself with worry over poor Althea, but I wondered about it later. Now I will cease holding a grudge for your absence."

He could hear the smile in her voice even though he avoided looking at her.

"I appreciate your forgiveness."

She gurgled with laughter over his dry tone.

"You can be remarkably entertaining, doctor. I would never have known."

"I think, perhaps, you might just be overcome with your exhaustion at this point. Everything seems to be setting you off into peals of laughter." His comment met with more laughter from her.

"You could be right, doctor. I am not usually subject to such fits and giggles. I do hope I am not causing you offense. I don't mean to be laughing at you, you do realize, don't you?"

"Of course. But I do wish you could be so well amused in my company when you are fully rested and in full possession of your wits."

⚘

His statement was met with silence while he wondered himself where his words had come from. *What was he thinking to make such a leading statement? Did he really want the woman's attention?*

"Why is that, doctor?"

"Surely by now you could call me Wyatt, couldn't you? We *have* spent the last three days saving two lives. Does that not qualify as the means for getting us past such formality?"

Katie had stopped in her tracks, so he was forced to turn around and face her. He raised the lantern to better make out her features and try to gauge her reaction. She blinked at the sudden brightness, but it also seemed as though she were trying to blink away her confusion, too.

"I suppose you are right, doctor, or Wyatt, I suppose. But do you think we are to be friends? Will it not cause gossip to spread about us if I were to suddenly start calling you by your first name?"

"What sort of gossip?" he asked, wondering where she would go with her line of reasoning. He was rewarded by a becoming blush staining her cheeks.

"The townspeople will think we're courting."

"Would that be so bad?" he asked her and himself at the same time.

She blinked again. "Doctor Jeffries," she began, trying to sound severe, showing that her familiarity was short lived. "I do believe I am much too tired for this conversation. If I had all my faculties, I am sure I would be horrified at the thought of people thinking we were courting. But right now, it doesn't feel nearly as bad as it should." She giggled again before adding, "I feel as though I have had a touch too much cordial despite not having had a single drop." She set off again. "Do hurry up, Wyatt. I am nearly falling over and am surely in need of my bed."

Wyatt grinned and trotted after her.

Chapter Thirteen

The next morning, Katie woke up suddenly from a sound sleep with a gasp. *Good heavens, did I proposition the doctor?* she asked herself. From the light streaming into her room, it was certain that many hours had passed. She was actually feeling remarkably rested despite all she had been through in the past several days. Throwing back the covers, Katie hopped out of bed, the need for action spurring her on.

After hastily donning clean clothes and scrubbing her face, Katie hurried from her room.

"Good morning, sleepy head. I was beginning to wonder if I needed to send for the doctor. It is so unlike you to sleep late."

Katie started at the mention of Doctor Jeffries. "Why would you send for him?" she demanded, worry and suspicion ringing in her voice.

Melanie laughed. "What's up with you? Did you wake up on the wrong side of the bed?"

A part of Katie wanted to stick her tongue out at Melanie, but she couldn't help but laugh along with her. "Maybe I did," she admitted. "I slept like a log, so there's no excuse for being grumpy. But I sure needed it. I have never felt so tired as I did last night when I crawled into bed."

"I'm glad you slept well. You weren't making total sense when you got home."

Katie could feel color creeping up her cheeks, but she managed to keep her response mild. "Oh, why do you say that?"

"You were giggling so much I couldn't get much out of you while I was helping you change into your nightgown. You were admonishing me not to burn your gown, as though you thought I actually might do so."

Katie had to giggle again over this. "I had actually told Doctor Jeffries that I felt I ought to burn it after having been in it nonstop for so long. I'm glad you saw I wasn't making sense."

"You were also babbling something about gossip and courting. I couldn't get you to explain yourself, you were too far gone in your giggles and being half asleep already. I do have this to say for you. You don't get mean when you're incoherent, at least."

Katie giggled again. "I suppose that's good to know. I'm sorry you had to deal with me in that state. I really was beside myself with exhaustion. That's the only explanation I have."

Melanie waved her words away. "No apologies necessary. It was kind of cute. And actually, a little reassuring. You are always so competent and together. Seeing you a little unhinged made you seem mortal."

"Melanie Jones, of course I'm mortal. And normal. And *far* from competent, I can assure you." Then with a cheeky grin she added, "But I'm glad to know I have everyone fooled most of the time."

The two friends shared more laughter before Melanie sobered enough to cast Katie a speculative glance. "But I'm still left wondering why you reacted so strongly to me saying I should send for the doctor. And when I add that in with remembering your mumblings last night, I have to ask, are you concerned there will be gossip about you and the doctor being cooped up with the Mitchells? Because I can assure you, from what I could glean from the townspeople I encountered while out with Annie, everyone only had good things to say about you being so kind to the Mitchells. And Matt was there the whole time, besides the Mitchells being an older, married couple. Surely there was nothing improper in the least."

Katie was shaking her head but couldn't keep her blush at bay. "No, no. I know no one will think it was improper. Well, no one in their right mind, at the very least."

"Then why are your cheeks suddenly so rosy then?"

Katie huffed and sat down at the table, accepting the cup of tea Melanie had prepared for her. "Doctor Jeffries told me to call him

Wyatt. I thought that would give rise to gossip. I told him so. And apparently I was still going on about it when I got home."

"Well, with what you went through together, I guess it would seem silly and pretentious to remain formal with the man. I don't think it would give rise to gossip, Katie. Everyone would surely understand." She paused before turning widening eyes on her. "But being in such close quarters with a man would surely lead to warm feelings developing between him and a healthy young woman. Katie Carter, are you courting with the doctor?"

Katie felt as though her entire body was probably red. "No, I am not," she protested.

"Then why are you blushing from tip to toes?" Melanie asked with a laugh.

"I'm embarrassed by your question, if you must know. Surely you remember me telling you I have no intention of ever remarrying."

"I do remember you saying such a daft thing. Katie, you're young, healthy, and vibrant. And you have a child. I know you love children. I've seen you with the orphans. You can't tell me you wouldn't like to have more. Even a little baby. Doesn't every woman want a baby of her own?"

Katie wanted to protest, but her heart softened at her friend's words, wondering how much of them were directed toward her and how much she was speaking of her own desires. Katie squeezed the other woman's hand and they were silent for a moment.

Breaking the silence, Katie said, "Babies and children are not the only thing you get from a marriage. You get stuck with a husband. That is not always such a fun thing."

"That's when you need a good solid cast iron skillet," Melanie responded swiftly.

Katie's mouth hung open and only laughter could emerge. "You might have a point there, my dear friend," she finally gasped when she was able to control her laughter to a degree.

Melanie's eyes lit up. "So you'll consider the doctor?"

"I didn't say that, now did I? Can you imagine? We have already made so many changes in our lives in the past weeks and months. Starting our new lives out here in Missouri. I have a daughter. And are you really trying to get rid of me? What would you do in this little house all by yourself without Annie and me to keep you company?"

Melanie grinned back at her. "Of course I'm not trying to get rid of you, but don't ever let me stand in the way of your happiness, either. You and Annie deserve the very best in life."

"And you think the doctor is the best?"

Melanie shrugged. "I think it would be best for you to have a mate and for Annie to have a father," she said as lightly as she could before laughing again. "And imagine only having to do the dishes for one person."

Katie threw a dish towel at her while they laughed together in friendship.

They had the small house fresh and shining in short order. When there was a light knock at the door, Katie glanced at the clock. "I thought Mary's dad was bringing Annie home after lunch today," she commented as she hurried to the door, anxious to see her daughter.

She blinked in surprise when she saw it was Doctor Jeffries. Feeling color mounting in her cheeks, she offered him a shy smile. "Good day, Wyatt," she said, barely above a whisper.

"You look none the worse for wear," he answered her cheerfully.

Katie suddenly thought of something, and she felt the flush seeping from her cheeks. "Is everything all right with the Mitchells? Do you need my help again? You should have sent Matt." Her voice was rising with each phrase, and Wyatt chuckled.

"Hush now, everything is fine. I just wanted to check on you."

Now Katie frowned at him. "Should you have left them on their own like this?"

Wyatt's grin didn't falter. They were on the front porch of her small house. Katie's frown deepened. "Are you all right, doctor? You probably didn't have as restful a night as I did."

"You are a worrier, aren't you?" His tone was teasing but kind.

Katie shrugged. "Sometimes."

"The Mitchells are on the mend, I swear to you. I managed not to burn the eggs I fried up for them this morning, and they ate with remarkably improved appetite, I am relieved to report to you. I will continue to nurse them a day or two longer as I don't want to risk anyone else coming into contact with them when they might still be contagious. Fortunately for them, you left their house in such a good state, that I shouldn't be able to run it completely aground before Mrs. Mitchell is back on her feet."

Katie was able to smile at this. "And how is Matt faring? The poor boy was nearly beside himself with worry for a while there."

"He, too, is much improved. He was actually running around chasing cats this morning when I left, and Mr. and Mrs. Mitchell were sleeping deeply. I'll be hard pressed to keep them in bed much longer, I'm sure. Especially Mr. Mitchell. Matt has been doing well about looking after the animals, but I know Mr. Mitchell will want to see for himself, maybe even by the end of the day today. Which is why I took this opportunity to come and see you. I'll most likely have to stand guard over them for the rest of the day, so I'll be confined."

Katie chuckled. "They seemed to be a rather meek couple. I don't think you'll have much trouble."

"You've only seen them ill. Wait until you get to know them when they're well. You might have a change of opinion."

Katie laughed again. "I look forward to making their acquaintance then."

"Oh yes, Mrs. Mitchell was asking about you over breakfast. She was sorely disappointed about messing up her appointment with you."

Katie eyed him askance. "Are you making fun of me now, doctor?"

"Why would I do that?"

"Surely the poor woman isn't considering fashion at a time like this."

"Even sick women can be vain," he observed.

Katie went off in a peel of laughter. "And isn't it good for me and Melanie that that is true? If it comes up again, assure Mrs. Mitchell that I will be happy to return when she is back on her feet."

"She'll be relieved to hear it."

They shared a smile before Katie averted her eyes and briskly asked, "Was that what you came to tell me?"

Wyatt's laugh was a little more awkward this time. "No, actually, I have managed to talk all around the bush and haven't gotten anywhere near my point. Would you be so kind as to take a stroll with me? That might help."

Katie's frown returned, but then she caught her breath as he reached out to touch the small furrow between her brows. "Don't frown, my dear, I promise it's nothing dire."

The butterflies in her stomach were starting to feel more like turkeys lumbering around her midsection. Katie tried to shake off the nerves, but there wasn't much she could do about it. She licked her lips and smoothed her hands over her skirt.

"Well, I have a little bit of time before Annie is due to return, and I'm fairly sure my chores are looked after for now. Besides, you probably don't have overly much time anyway. So, I will stroll with you. But mind you, we cannot go far. I have no wish to set the town's tongues to wagging."

By the time she had managed to stop herself from babbling all this out, they were already well on their way. Katie was feeling slightly mortified about all the words she had allowed to tumble from her lips and couldn't make herself make eye contact with her companion. They strode along in silence for a few minutes. It felt like hours to her, but she was fairly certain it might not have even been three minutes. Maybe not even two. Surely she was losing her mind. She tried not to fidget, but finally she couldn't take it anymore.

"Where are we going?"

"There's a lovely spot along this trail a ways," he said. "It's a little bit of a trek since it's up a small hill, but I think you'll agree that the view is worth it."

Katie finally glanced at him. "You are enjoying living out here, aren't you?"

"I really am. I cannot say for certain that I would never want to move back East, but I really don't think I will want to leave these parts. The beauty is astounding, not at all what I would have expected, and not what I would have thought would appeal to me, since Boston was what I always knew. But there's just something so appealing about the freedom and wildness of these parts."

"I know what you mean," Katie agreed. "While I was anxious for a fresh start, I didn't think I would come to love it out here like I do. I thought I was a city girl through and through. But it's quite amazing how exhilarating fresh air and trees can be."

They shared a friendly chuckle as they neared the top of the rise, and then Katie's breath caught as she took in the spectacle before her. It was green as far as she could see with very little to mar the landscape. A few small houses could be seen in the distance with some cows and sheep dotting the fields and a few trees lining the creek that meandered through the vista. The sunshine was warm on her shoulders, and the fresh smell was sweet and clean.

Katie finally broke the quiet. "I think it would take me decades to tire of this view."

"I agree," Wyatt said.

But he was looking at her, not at the scenery, and Katie could feel warmth creeping toward her scalp as the nerves that had dissipated while they walked returned in full force. She began to fidget once more.

"Thank you for sharing this with me. I'm a little surprised, though, that you would take the time to do so, since you must surely be fully occupied with your patients."

Wyatt shrugged. "I didn't want to visit any of my other patients just yet, in case I might be carrying the Mitchells' illness. So far, I haven't seemed to develop any symptoms, so hopefully I share your immunity."

"Well that's fortunate," she replied.

"Yes," he began, but she spoke at the same time and interrupted him.

"I ought to get back. Annie is supposed to be coming home after lunch, and I haven't seen her for days. I wouldn't want her to fret if I'm absent."

Wyatt put his hand out and stilled her fidgeting fingers. "Just a moment, Katie, I'm trying to discuss something with you."

Katie's stomach turned over in a manner that she thought might be pleasant if she could get her mind to return to functioning. As it was, all she could do was stand still and blink at him and absorb the delicious sensation of having his warm hands engulfing her own.

"I know I have been rather obnoxious in the past in my opinions about independent women. I think I owe you an apology."

Disappointment swept through her, which she considered to be completely irrational. She wished she could wave her hand nonchalantly. But since it was still clasped in his, Katie tried for a breezy tone as she said, "Please, think nothing of it. I didn't allow it to weigh on me."

"That is certainly a relief," he said with a wide smile. "I wouldn't want you to be offended with me."

"Of course not, with us both being rather public people, our paths are sure to cross from time to time. It wouldn't do for us to be at loggerheads."

"No, it most certainly would not do." His voice was strained, and Katie wondered if he was laughing at her, but she again couldn't bring herself to meet his gaze. He continued, "You see, Katie, I was thinking that I would rather our paths more than crossed from time to time. I may not have been clear in my intentions, but I would quite like it if we shared the same path, if you know what I mean."

"I don't reckon that I do know what you mean, Wyatt," Katie answered, feeling as though her emotions were in a windstorm as they tossed about from one direction to another. "Won't it cause gossip if we take many walks together?"

Wyatt chuckled. "Not if you would agree to me courting you."

Katie gasped. "Courtship? Wyatt Jeffries, are you making fun of me again?"

Now Wyatt was left blinking at her. "Why would you think I'm making fun? I'm trying to engage your interest."

Katie went off in a peel of laughter. "Melanie will have a great laugh over this."

"This isn't going exactly how I had envisioned," Wyatt commented blandly.

"You envisioned this?" Katie asked, feeling a little breathless once more.

"I did."

"How did it go in your vision?"

"Well, you didn't consider it a joke. In fact, you thought it was a brilliant idea and flung your arms around my neck announcing your instant agreement."

"Seems like your imagination might not know me so well."

Wyatt chuckled. "A man is allowed to dream, Katie Carter." His tone was dry, but there was still a twinkle in his eye. "I realize this might seem sudden to you. I didn't want to declare myself as we were hovering over the Mitchells' sick bed."

"I can see that would be remarkably bad form," Katie agreed with a grin.

"Quite right. But I find that while I have a remarkably good imagination, I cannot envision a future that does not contain you in it, by my side, sharing my life, even helping me with my patients, or pursuing your own interests," he was quick to add, "whatever you think best, as long as you return home each night to share your thoughts and dreams with me and whatever family we manage to grow together."

Katie felt tears gather in her eyes. "That sounds wonderful, Wyatt." Suddenly though, she grew sober once more. "The only trouble is, this is all rather sudden, wouldn't you say? Just days ago we weren't sure if we could even bear each other."

"I knew I could bear you, Katie, I was just afraid."

Katie smiled over that admission, but continued, "The thing is, Wyatt, I'm a mother now, and I cannot only think of myself. Annie hasn't been along for the journey of us coming to this understanding. She has to be my first priority. And I need to make sure that she's all right with these changes. If I agree, you'll have to understand that you need to court the both of us."

Wyatt studied her seriously for a heartbeat before he broke into a grin. "I rather think that sounds like double the pleasure.

Katie then surprised him by throwing her arms around his neck. "Well then, I think I might have to quickly agree."

With a whoop of joy, Wyatt twirled her around while she laughed with delight. Finally, allowing her to sink down to her feet, he bent his head and sealed their bargain with a sweet kiss.

Epilogue

Katie was standing nervously in the spot where Wyatt had asked her to meet him. The exact place where he had declared himself two months prior. She was amazed how patiently he had courted her and Annie. She herself would have thought he needn't have taken quite so much time. Anyone could see that both she and Annie were head over heels about him. But he had been true to his word. He had taken his time with Annie, allowing her to get over her distrust of doctors. And he had lovingly allowed Katie time to get over her distrust of men. She had come to anticipate the sound of his knock each evening as he called by, even sometimes just for a moment or two, just to say hello and see how her and Annie's day had been. She knew it must have been exhausting for him after his long days of caring for others. But it had gone a long way to help both of his "girls" arrive at the conclusion that they couldn't imagine their lives without him in it.

But it had already been a couple of weeks since Katie had arrived at that realization. She was beginning to wonder if she was going to have to propose to him, she thought with a grin as she gazed out at the beautiful vista in front of her. She was beginning to grow impatient with the good doctor. Both in this moment of waiting for him — surely he was late for their appointment — and with this courtship. She was ready to get on with their new life together.

A sound behind her drew her attention. When she turned to look, tears almost clogged her throat. Wyatt was walking toward her, hand-in-hand with Annie. Annie was carrying a beautiful, enormous bouquet of flowers that surely must have taken ages to gather. That would account for the delay, she thought with a grin. Then she realized that Wyatt was carrying a shovel and she frowned in confusion.

"Well this is a pleasant surprise," she greeted them as Annie ran toward her. "Thank you, Annie, these are beautiful."

"They're from both of us. Because we love you," Annie said, making the tears swimming in Katie's eyes tumble down her cheeks. "That's s'posed to make you happy, not cry," Annie pointed out, becoming distressed.

Katie laughed. "Sometimes tears can be from happiness, not just for sadness." Annie looked slightly mollified but still somewhat skeptical. Her attention was quickly turned, though, when Wyatt gained their attention.

"Annie, please stand there with Katie. I have something important I want to discuss with the both of you."

Katie's heart thudded in her chest, and she felt momentarily light-headed as her mind filled with hope. But she couldn't help grinning over the wide-eyed confusion on Annie's face. The tears that had dried were soon joined by more as Wyatt crouched down onto one knee in order to be on the same level with Annie.

"Annie, my dear girl, I hope you realize how truly special you have become to me. I know you have faced many challenges already in your young life, and it has taken a great deal of courage to allow me into your life. I think you're the bravest little girl I have ever met. And I was wondering if you would be willing to make it a permanent arrangement."

The child blinked, staring at the doctor without fully understanding his meaning. Wyatt quickly elaborated.

"I know no one can ever replace the mother and father you lost, and I know you have made a new life with Katie, but would you be willing to allow me to join that life, so that we could all live together?"

"So we can be together every day, and you don't have to go home by yourself?"

"Exactly right. I don't want to go home by myself anymore."

The little girl stared at him solemnly. "I don't like being by myself either. If Katie says it's all right, I think it's a good idea."

Wyatt grinned; his gaze flicked up to Katie for a second, but he kept his focus on Annie while he pointed into the distance. "Would you mind going over there to play for a few minutes while I discuss it with Katie?"

"All right," she agreed and scampered off.

"Well, Katie, you can now see that my future loneliness or companionship comes down to your say so," he remarked as they both watched Annie skipping in the field. Turning to her, Wyatt gathered up her hands. "Katie, darling, I have tried to take my time and allow the two of you to grow accustomed to me, but I don't think I can wait any longer. I love the both of you more than life itself. Please, tell me you'll put me out of my misery and become my wife."

Katie burst into laughter. "I thought you'd never ask!"

"What? I've been nearly consumed with impatience for weeks."

"You hid it well, Dr. Jeffries." Katie's reply was arch.

He gathered her into his arms. "Are you really going to marry me?"

Katie smiled. "I really am."

He twirled her around, and their laughter mingled. "How soon can we manage it?"

Katie's laughter rang out louder. "From taking your time, now you're impatient?"

Wyatt was rueful. "Do you mind terribly? Do you want to wait for friends or family to come from New York?"

Katie quickly denied that. "Not at all. I have no need for a big wedding. In fact, I am as impatient as you. Maybe even more so. I love you, too, Wyatt, and will happily marry you as soon as it can be arranged."

They laughed together before Wyatt silenced them both as he stole her breath with a tender kiss.

The End

Read the next book in the *Orphan Train* series,

Melanie

Two challenged hearts. One true love?

Stay in touch with Wendy May Andrews and forthcoming publishing news.

Sign up for her biweekly newsletter on wendymayandrews.com

Married by Proxy

Another series set in the mid-west you will love:

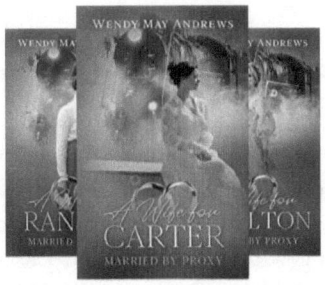

They didn't meet until after the wedding day.

Carter McLain has finally accomplished the success he was striving for when he moved to the frontier a decade ago. All that's missing is a wife to share it with. Having no desire to leave his land, he requests a friend back home to arrange a proxy marriage for him. When his bride seems too good to be true, Carter wonders if he did the right thing.

The highly publicized deaths of Ella St. Clair's parents cause her to lose everything. Left destitute, alone, and friendless, she grudgingly accepts the offer of marriage by proxy to a man she has never met. The long trip West leaves her plenty of time for second thoughts.

What does the future hold for these legally bound strangers? Can they get past their secrets to find happiness?

This is a sweet, wholesome historical romance featuring a smart, strong heroine and the brooding hero who steals her heart. Download today and get ready to fall in love.

To buy please visit wendymayandrews.com

About the Author

I've been writing pretty much since I learned to read when I was five years old. Of course, those early efforts were basically only something a mother could love ☺ I put writing aside after I left school and stuck with reading. I am an avid reader. I love words. I will read anything, even the cereal box, signs, posters, etc. But my true love is novels.

Almost ten years ago my husband dared me to write a book instead of always reading them. I didn't think I'd be able to do it, but to my surprise I love writing. Those early efforts eventually became my first published book – *Tempting the Earl* (published by Avalon books in 2010). There were some ups and downs in my publishing efforts. My first publisher was sold and I became an "orphan" author, back to the drawing board of trying to find a publishing house. It has been a thrilling adventure as I learned to navigate the world of publishing.

I believe firmly that everyone deserves a happily ever after. I want my readers to be able to escape from the everyday for a little while and feel upbeat and refreshed when they get to the end of my books.

When not reading or writing, I can be found traipsing around my neighborhood admiring the dogs and greenery or travelling the world with my favorite companion.

Stay in touch:

Website: www.wendymayandrews.com

Facebook: www.facebook.com/WendyMayAndrews

Instagram: www.instagram.com/WendyMayAndrews

Twitter: www.twitter.com/WendyMayAndrews